Hoofbeats

Lara and the Silent Place

Book Four

by KATHLEEN DUEY

D0096936

PUFFIN BOOKS

PUFFIN BOOKS
Published by the Penguin Group
Penguin Young Readers Group, 345 Hudson Street,
New York, New York 10014, U.S.A.
Penguin Group (Canada), 10 Alcorn Avenue, Toronto, Ontario,
Canada M4V 3B2 (a division of Pearson Penguin Canada Inc.)
Penguin Books Ltd, 80 Strand, London WC2R 0RL, England
Penguin Ireland, 25 St Stephen's Green, Dublin 2, Ireland
(a division of Penguin Books Ltd)
Penguin Group (Australia), 250 Camberwell Road, Camberwell,
Victoria 3124, Australia (a division of Pearson Australia Group Pty Ltd)
Penguin Books India Pvt Ltd, 11 Community Centre,
Panchsheel Park, New Delhi - 110 017, India
Penguin Group (NZ), Cnr Airborne and Rosedale Roads, Albany,
Auckland 1310, New Zealand (a division of Pearson New Zealand Ltd)
Penguin Books (South Africa) (Pty) Ltd, 24 Sturdee Avenue,
Rosebank, Johannesburg 2196, South Africa

Penguin Books Ltd, Registered Offices: 80 Strand,
London WC2R 0RL, England

Published simultaneously in the United States of America by Dutton Children's
Books and Puffin Books, divisions of Penguin Young Readers Group, 2005

1 3 5 7 9 10 8 6 4 2

Copyright © Kathleen Duey, 2005
All rights reserved.

Puffin Books ISBN 0-14-240233-8

Printed in the United States of America

For Star, a dapple-gray Welsh pony, with a true five-point white star on his side. He was the smartest pony I have ever known. I met him in a dark pasture, in a driving rain, on the night he was born. Birth is a fierce, joyous miracle. Anyone who falls in love with a newborn foal is permanently touched, forever changed, forever grateful.

CHAPTER ONE

❧ ❧ ❧

*I was tired and I did not like the noise. People pressed
close and it frightened me. But my mother's gentle
hands and soft voice reassured me as she guided
me through the crowds.*

*R*iding away from Athenry Castle, I kept
Dannsair to an ambling walk. It was the
only way that we could escape, as strange as that
might seem.

Had we galloped through the crowd of people
celebrating Beltaine—all of them joyous that
summer had finally begun—someone would have
noticed us. As it was, only one or two bothered to
so much as glance at my filly and me—and then
without much interest. They could not know that
I was not what I seemed to be.

My Dannsair was only a yearling, tall and strong, but she was often silly and flighty, as befitted her age. As spirited as she was, keeping her to a walk would have been hard on any other day.

Very hard.

That day, it was easy, even though the meadow was noisy and crowded. She was just plain weary. We had won a race early that morning—a long and difficult race against older horses and older riders. It should have been the most perfect day of my life.

It wasn't.

The sun was passing its midday height as I guided Dannsair along the edge of the wide meadow, my stomach knotted and my hand unsteady. The sky was clear and bright, so people were starting cookfires in order to boil the day's meat, eggs, and barley. I saw a woman milking her cow near the tents, spancels fixed around the animal's front legs to keep it from running off.

The crowd in the meadow included horses and dogs as well as a scattering of chickens and milk cows that had been brought along to provide milk and meat for the travelers. People were walking in groups, retelling what they had seen of the morning's race. They talked about their wagers, and it sounded to me as though no one had bet on us. No one had thought the moon-colored filly could win.

We had earned our victory, I tell you true. I had ridden Dannsair hard in the race, both of us giving every bit of our strength and will to win. I had risked hurting her, riding her that way, but I had believed the stablemaster. He told me that if we won, I could take my filly as my prize instead of the gold that the Baron of Athenry had promised would be mine.

That was my dream, and it had been since Dannsair's birth. I wanted her to be my own, never to be used in battle, for both of us to live a happy and peaceful life.

Thinking about the baron's broken promise made me so angry that I bit my lower lip to still my fury. How could any man be so cruel? It was a certainty that the stablemaster knew how much I loved Dannsair. He had watched me work with her, had seen how we trusted each other. Yet he had helped the baron betray me. Perhaps it had been his idea. I hoped I never had to see either man again. Ever.

I was Dannsair's mother, in an odd way. I had raised her from the moment she had been born because her dam had died bearing her. So Dannsair had always looked to me to protect her and care for her.

And now that she was older, she trusted me on her back, relied on me to guide her over rough ground and not to ask her to do anything that would hurt her. And yet I *had* risked hurting us both because I had been foolish enough to believe a lie. I was angry with myself.

As I rode beside the town wall, I kept glancing back toward the North Gate. It was only a matter of time before the stablemaster noticed that Dannsair was not in her stall. It could happen any moment, but with luck, it would not. If the baron's Feast of Beltaine—the celebration full of honeyed mead and roast venison—was long and loud, no one would be checking the barns until tomorrow morning.

When the stablemaster did notice, he would search, I was sure. He would be desperate to find

Dannsair. If we managed to get well away before he saw us, our chances of disappearing were fairly good, or so I hoped.

He would ask who had seen us, of course, but he would be asking after a Norman boy named Trian and a moon-hued filly. And Dannsair and I weren't either of those things. Not anymore.

Dannsair's coat was dyed brown now, thanks to Old Brigit's pots of bogberry powder. And I didn't look like a Norman boy anymore. My hair was growing out, braided beneath a laced hood, and I was wearing Old Brigit's blue-green wedding dress, the full skirt draped over Dannsair's hindquarters. Beneath it was a carry sack.

My cloak, my two linen leinte—one old and one nearly new—and the beautiful little gold pin I had found at home were in it. So were a few balls of hard cheese and oatcakes Brigit had given me. I would not be hungry for a while at least.

The people I recognized from Athenry probably thought I was some strange Norman girl who had come from Galway with her family to see the horse race. The Irish people who had come would think I lived in Athenry—if anyone bothered to have a thought about me at all.

Once we were past most of the crowd, my stomach knots loosened a little and I began to listen to what people around us were saying. Dannsair was content to walk slowly, carrying her head lower than usual, her tail switching at the noontime flies.

"A yearling filly," I heard one man say, shaking his head. "Just a yearling and she beat them all."

I pressed my lips together to keep from smiling. I fixed my eyes straight ahead and rode slowly, as though I had nowhere at all to go.

Then, as Dannsair carried me quietly along the edge of the crowds, I saw Cormac at a distance. He turned and looked my way. I felt his gaze like the touch of a hand on my shoulder, and I looked away, quickly, hoping he had not recognized me dressed as a Norman boy in the race. He couldn't know that I had followed Dannsair here, to Athenry town. He would not be looking for me.

I kept my face turned away from Cormac and rode on, holding my breath, hoping he would not know me, or, if he did, that he would not call out.

I wished I could just go talk to him.

Cormac had known me for what I truly was—an Irish girl from a poor tuath who wore plain leinte woven from flax thread with long, unruly hair and a love for horses that I could not hide. He had liked me enough to help me try to escape. He had known Dannsair as herself, too—a tall, graceful filly the color of the moon, as she had looked in the race that very morning.

I knew he wouldn't recognize her at this distance, through the crowds and commotion, her coat dyed bogberry brown. So long as nothing set him wondering and he did not make a point of getting closer.

So I rode on.

I glanced back only once, veering toward the woods. When I did, Cormac was no longer looking my way. I was both relieved and disappointed.

This was the truth:

I liked Cormac a great deal. I liked him in that silly flushed-cheeks way that I had always made fun of—and never would again. I couldn't, not now that I understood how it felt. He had been very kind to me, and had given Dannsair her name.

I hoped I would see him again one day, even though he had once caused me trouble without meaning to. But in all likelihood, I would not.

At the top of the meadow, my heart bumping against my ribs, I reined in a moment, then turned Dannsair into the woods. We passed the holly tree I had used as a watcher's perch the autumn before.

No one shouted after us. No one cared at all where a Norman girl and her drab-brown filly were going during the Feast of Beltaine.

The voices in the meadow dimming behind us, I guided Dannsair toward the creek where I had bathed, near where I had helped Niall find his pigs. I owed him a debt for telling me that the baron was not going to give me Dannsair. But more than anyone, I owed Old Brigit for taking me in and feeding me, giving me a real home during my stay inside Athenry's stone walls.

I would miss her, and I would always wish her well. It was a shame she had no children of her own; she was as loving as any mother could have been.

I gently reined in again at the creek's edge,

then slackened the reins so that Dannsair could get a long drink of the cool water. I did not dismount, even though I was fairly sure that we were safe, at least for a time.

But whether the stablemaster discovered Dannsair's empty stall today or in the morning at his usual time, he would be furious. It would not take him long to find out that I was gone as well. Then he would send men to find us.

After a long drink of the cool water, Dannsair took a half step forward, then another, tossing her head. She pawed at the creek bed, splashing. I knew what she wanted. The cool, shallow water would be perfect for a belly-splashing horse bath.

"No, please," I told her. "I don't know how well the dye will stay in your coat."

But Dannsair ignored me and pawed at the water, wetting her underside and the hem of Old Brigit's dress. I nudged her forward, pulling hard on one rein. She turned in a tight circle, and I exhaled in relief as she waded out and walked up the grassy bank. I would have to be more careful when she drank, and I could only pray that it would not rain hard.

I wasn't sure how well the bogberry dye would work. If the mud-brown color were to wash out of her coat, it would be much harder to get away from Athenry without being recognized—for Dannsair, especially. She and her sire were the only two moon-colored horses I had ever seen anywhere.

"By the time they come looking," I told Dannsair as we started uphill into the forest, "we will be long gone."

Then I gently tightened my legs against her sides and urged her into an easy jog-trot. I knew how tired she was, but we had to put some distance between us and Athenry Castle before nightfall.

Dannsair rose into the gait gracefully, switching her long tail to let me know that she would rather roll in the cool water, and then have a nap in the sun. But, as always, she understood what I needed her to do, and she did it for me, even though it made no sense to her.

Dannsair loved me, and I loved her. Riding away from Athenry Castle, I clung to that. I had nothing else to cling to. I was a long way from my home, and I had no idea at all where we were going.

CHAPTER TWO

✤ ✤ ✤

*The woods were quiet and smelled of new grass and
new leaves. I could tell that my mother was afraid of
something, but I could not tell what. There was no
scent of wolves, no sign of any danger at all.*

*T*hat night I camped only a little before
the sunrise began the new day. I had
spent every moment of the day listening for what
I feared most—hoofbeats and voices behind us.
But none came.

Dannsair was so tired that she barely grazed
before she lay down in the grass. I didn't take off
the bridle I had made for her. There was no bit,
and the straps were all woven wool—flat, wide,
and soft, so I knew it wouldn't chafe her skin.
And here is the truth: I was afraid to take it off.

I was very glad to stretch out on the grass myself. I lay awake long after I could hear my filly's slow, even breathing. I wasn't sure she would stay as close to me as she had last summer. She was much older now and had gotten used to being confined in a stall most of the time.

And there was this:

Dannsair had less and less use for a foster mother, even though she loved me still. This was natural and the way it was for all horses. As they grow into adulthood, they stay closer to the young horses their own age rather than trailing after their mothers all the time.

I slept only a little. Every rustle in the woods made me listen, my whole body tense.

What if something scared Dannsair and she galloped off? I finally wrapped the reins around my wrist so that if she woke and stood, it would wake me. It was foolish, I knew. If she was truly terrified, she might drag me or trample me in the dark. But I couldn't imagine her hurting me, and I could not stand the idea of her getting away.

The next morning was bright and sunny. I listened to the pattering sound of a woodpecker drilling his way into alder bark. I heard the music of the creek we had followed much of the day before. And I heard the deep silence of the trees and the stone that underlay it all.

In the town of Athenry, there were few birds. There were, indeed, more people than anything else. I had gotten used to voices and the commotion of people working. I had forgotten the peaceful quiet of the woods.

Dannsair and I traveled westward that day, straight away from the rising sun. I had no particular reason to go that way except this one: It was more or less the direction of my home.

But that was foolish. My home—my dear double-walled rath and the houses that held my friends and family—was the one place on this earth that I could not go.

The Baron of Athenry had been desperate to win the race, especially against Irish horses. His stablemaster had told me the baron would keep his prize of gold and give me my Dannsair instead if I won the race for him.

I *had* won, but he had never intended to keep his word. He would try to get Dannsair back. And worse, eventually, the stablemaster would talk to Conall or to Cormac's father about the moon-colored filly they had traded to the baron. Dannsair was of rare breeding, and the baron had been very interested in her bloodlines.

When Conall and Cormac's father were told the filly had disappeared and a stable boy with her, they might also be told that the "boy" had trained her, that she had obeyed without halter or bridle, and that a complete trust had been obvious between horse and rider.

Conall would easily guess from a description that the boy was, in fact, me. After all, he had seen me working with Dannsair since she was wobbly on her legs. If he told the baron, he would know *where* to look for Dannsair. He would come to my tuath. No Norman baron would tolerate being bested by an Irish girl.

I sighed.

The risk was too great. As much as I wanted to go home, I could not put my family in danger.

The next day, with me still wearing Old Brigit's dress and Dannsair still wearing the woven Norman saddle she had given us, we came upon a wide road that led westward. We traveled at a canter all morning.

When the sun was high, we stopped near a creek so Dannsair could graze and I could eat cheese and oatcakes. The grass was rich and deep, and Dannsair cut greedy mouthfuls with her teeth, her jaw working steadily from the moment we stopped until I was ready to go on.

For the rest of the day, I cantered Dannsair until her breathing was quick, then pulled her back to a jog until it steadied and quieted. I kept my head up, listening and watching the woods on both sides of us. Dannsair's speed would be our only hope of escape if the baron's men appeared.

It was nearly evening when I heard hoofbeats. Dannsair tossed her head and tried to turn to face the sound. I pulled her around in a circle and got her moving into the woods. By the time the horsemen cantered past, we were standing behind a thicket of wild plum.

I could see them well enough as they passed. They were dressed to fight, in the Norman fashion. They carried shields and swords, and their faces were grim and tight as they rode.

They were from Athenry, I was nearly sure. I had seen many men there with the same designs on their tunics, anyway. I did not recognize any of them, but that meant little. I had seen the Norman men only from a distance as they came in and out of the North Gate and the castle walls. I had been busy taking care of Dannsair and helping Old Brigit at first—then I had done little except practice for the race.

Dannsair did what she had been named for; she danced, her nostrils flared, her eyes bright.

Her dyed-drab coat would not catch anyone's eye, I was sure, but if she started whinnying, the men might rein in and come back to see who rode behind them—friend or foe. If they were from Athenry, they were looking for a boy on a cream-colored filly. But if they spoke to me and I had to answer, they would know instantly that I was not what I appeared to be.

I had my hand clasped over Dannsair's muzzle, and I was talking in her ear. "Don't whinny at them," I pleaded. "Not even if you know some of them from the baron's barns."

She shook her mane, and I lost my grip for a

second. She tossed her head high, and I took a step so that I stood directly in front of her. She was looking over my head. Her breathing quickened, and I knew she was about to whinny.

Desperate, I waved my arms to make her shy, then grabbed the bridle and pulled her around in circles to distract her.

She snorted and tossed her head again and then lowered her muzzle to nibble nervously at my hair.

"I am sorry," I whispered. "I didn't mean to scare you. But I couldn't let you betray us."

She shifted her weight and pawed at the earth. I had to step back or her hoof might have grazed my leg. "Dannsair?"

Her eyes were wide. She was staring at the woods where the riders had gone. I kept talking to her. She did calm down, but it took a long time. When I finally swung up onto her back, I left the road, using the last light of the sun to guide me. I swung northward, then headed west again. If the Normans came back the way they had gone, we would no longer be in their path.

Dannsair's longing to follow other horses

upset me. I knew she was growing up. I had so looked forward to riding her, to our galloping across the land and going where we pleased. It had not once occurred to me that Dannsair might want something different than I did. Walking with her beside me had come to feel as natural as walking with Bebinn or Gerroc back home. But now, after so many months spent in the Baron of Athenry's barns, she was more used to the company of other horses than to mine.

The day after we saw the riders, I set about finding out how much Dannsair remembered of the things I had taught her when she was a foal.

That meant I had to let her go free, which I was scared to do. The first time I tried it, I found a little clearing in the woods, bounded on two sides by tangled plum thickets. I left the bridle on her, but I tied the reins over her neck.

Then I took a single step backward. Dannsair watched me with her deep, dark eyes.

I took a second step.

Two steps. That was all I could bear to risk. I said her name in the singsong way she knew meant that she was to come to me.

She stepped forward without a second's hesitation. I exhaled in relief and worked up my courage to walk farther away from her. By midday, I was happy to know that she remembered all she had learned: She came when I called her name. Sometimes she would trot, sometimes she would canter, but she came, no matter whether I was ten steps away from her or fifty.

She would walk beside me without my holding the reins.

When I asked her to stay in one place while I walked away, then came back, she did it. I could tell that she liked this less than anything else, but she did it, for me.

That evening, I took the bridle off so that she could sleep easier, free to move about if she needed to. I was no longer afraid of her leaving me in the darkness. I knew that she wanted the company of other horses the way I wanted the company of my friends. But we still had each other, and we trusted each other. And for that I was more grateful than I can say.

CHAPTER THREE

❧ ❧ ❧

We traveled easy today, with my mother sitting straight and tall. I am rested and wanted to gallop more, but she held me in. At least there were horses to travel with and to stand with for warmth when the sun went down.

*W*e slept only a few hours each night, both of us restless and listening for danger. Dannsair grazed while I ate a little cheese, then we traveled on. One day, not long before dusk, I came around a long bend in the road and saw a procession of seven women wearing dark robes riding ahead of us.

It shocked me for a moment, to see them all riding with no men there to protect them. Their horses were plodding along so slowly that it was impossible to rein Dannsair in before we were nearly upon them.

I thought about veering off into the woods, but one of them made a gesture of greeting. Then the woman turned to her companions and said something I couldn't hear. In the next few seconds, all the women turned in their high-backed saddles and were smiling at me.

I stared at their dark robes and covered hair and finally realized what they were. Nuns. I had heard of them, of course, but had never seen any.

I reined Dannsair in. They would think me odd if I appeared to be afraid to come close to them. But then I realized my manner of speech would tell them I was Irish—and how would I explain my Norman clothing? I decided to ride straight past, smile, and not to say anything at all. I was not yet all that far from Athenry, and an Irish girl riding alone dressed as a Norman might be a tale retold if the baron came around looking for Dannsair.

As I fidgeted and held back, the women laughed at something, high and clear, like girls.

It made me homesick for Bebinn and Gerroc.

The woman at the front of the group turned in her saddle and beckoned me. I hesitated, reining Dannsair nearly to a halt. The woman stopped her horse, waiting for me. I was furious with myself. I should have simply ridden off into the woods. I smiled as best I could and tried simply to ride past.

It did not happen that way.

I don't know what I expected of nuns—a somber, prayerful demeanor, I suppose. They were more like a group of friendly women from some neighboring tuath.

"Hello!" the one in front called. I nodded politely and pulled Dannsair a little farther to one side. She was older than the rest of them. A few looked as young as my aunt Fallon—only four or five years older than I was.

"Is all well with you?" she asked me as I came close. I nodded and pretended to wave a fly off Dannsair's ears.

"Where are you bound?" she asked me. Her voice was sweet and kind.

I gestured westward and smiled again, urging Dannsair forward, but she resisted, and I knew why. She extended her neck and whickered at the horses. One or two answered her.

I didn't want to dig my heels into Dannsair's sides or make a show of urging her onward. I didn't want to give these nuns a single reason to remember me, to look at Dannsair or me too closely.

Dannsair lifted her head, walking almost sideways. I leaned forward, reining her back around to face the road straight on. She obeyed, in part. Her back end continued fairly straight, but her front end curved toward the horses again.

The nuns laughed at Dannsair's sidestepping and what probably looked like my embarrassment. It wasn't that. I was afraid. The nuns were all watching me, looking into my face. How could they not remember me now?

"Lovely little mare," one of them said. She had a round face and a wide smile.

I nodded.

"Is something wrong?" the nun at the front of the line asked me.

I shook my head.

"Maybe she's just fallen behind her traveling party," the round-faced nun said.

I nodded and gestured up the road. Then I pretended to fuss with the woven saddle.

"Our abbey is up that way," the woman at the front of the line said. "I am the abbess. If you are in need of our help . . . ?"

I shook my head, astonished at the kindness in her voice and her eyes. Just then, Dannsair jutted out her muzzle, trying to pull slack into the reins and sidled toward the horses again. They all laughed, louder this time.

"Your mare has a fine spirit," the abbess said. "One day we hope to help support the abbey by breeding horses. "We have talked our patrons out of two fine mares already, one in foal."

The round-faced woman nodded. "Mention our hopes to your father, will you please? Or to anyone who might give us a good mare or a colt to raise for our first stallion."

I nodded, knowing that it was a lie and that it had to be a special and terrible stain on my soul to lie to a nun. She thought I was the daughter of a wealthy Norman, and I was not. I was the daughter of a poor Irish rí who would no more give a stallion to nuns than the moon would shine green. I must have looked uneasy because the abbess frowned.

"Agnes means well," she said. "We don't mean to keep you from your journey." She looked into my eyes, and it felt to me as if she could see into my lonely, weary heart. "Unless you need a place to sleep safe this night?"

Without meaning to I nodded and my lips opened. "I do," I heard myself say. "Thank you."

If any of the nuns were surprised to hear a girl they had thought to be a Norman sound like a born-and-bred Irish girl, they did not show it. Instead, the abbess lifted her chin and smiled. Then she urged her old horse into a shuffling walk.

Dannsair loved traveling with the nuns. That is to say, she loved their horses. She arched her neck and pranced, nickering, impatient that none of them wanted to take a gallop with her. After a time, I cantered ahead, then turned and let her race back. After that, she was quieter.

"Did you train her?" the round-faced woman named Agnes asked me.

It was such an odd question.

I *had* of course. But girls didn't train horses. I looked into her eyes. She seemed perfectly serious. "Yes," I said cautiously.

"I thought so," she said. "You barely cue her. It's as though you know each other's minds."

I fell silent after that, afraid I would blurt out my whole story—I had never met anyone who understood horses the way I did.

Agnes smiled at me. "What else have you taught her?"

I hesitated, then described Dannsair coming when I called her, staying where I asked her to stay.

Agnes looked wistful. "Will you stay with us long enough to show me how you did that?"

"If the abbess doesn't mind, I will," I said.

"We welcome you," the abbess said.

I found myself smiling, relief washing through me like rain rinses grass. It seemed that Dannsair and I had found a safe place, at least for a time.

CHAPTER FOUR

❦ ❦ ❦

I like this place. It is quiet; no one shouts.
The horses are all content, the grass is
plentiful—and my mother is always happy.

*T*he abbey looked like a small tuath with a stone church at one end. It was not so grand as the church being built in Athenry town, but it was grand enough, with a fine tall cross of stone standing before the arched entrance. Between it and the long, low-roofed building where the nuns slept, there were well-tended gardens and a young apple orchard.

In a way, it was like coming home for me. The whole place was dotted with byres of wattle and daub as was my own tuath, the hardened mud walls covered with whitewash, the roof timbers squared with a hand ax. There were a few fields set off with arm-thick palings driven into the ground. And all was clean and well kept. The seedlings in their gardens were leaping out of the soil. It was lovely, *lovely*.

We arrived at last light. It was Agnes who insisted that Dannsair be turned loose with the other horses in their paling-enclosed pasture for the night. Dannsair hesitated only a moment before she leaped into the field, trotting.

It was Agnes who showed me my cot and helped me find a blanket to use. The abbess was kind enough to bring me barley water to warm me. I heard them saying their prayers, reciting a beautiful cascade of words I did not understand.

Morning was fresh and sunny, and I ran to see Dannsair. We played a little, her galloping circles around me. Then I turned to leave, to offer to do my share of the work, and I saw Agnes watching. Two other nuns were with her. Dannsair followed me to the gate in the palings.

"Oh, my, she is a beauty," Agnes sighed, patting Dannsair's neck. "What a fine head." She gently lifted Dannsair's muzzle and looked at her teeth. "What a fine length of leg for a yearling."

I glanced at her.

Agnes smiled. "She isn't two yet, is she?"

I shook my head and pressed my lips together. One thing was clear: Agnes knew horses.

"When I was little," she said, "all I wanted was to help with the horses. My father wouldn't hear of it. So here I am, and I might just get my way after all." She laughed, her high girlish laugh. Oh, how I envied her in that moment. Her dream was the same as my own—and she had found a way to make it come true.

That afternoon, I helped Agnes and Ann—another young nun—feed the horses. Most were plain stock, some of them old. All had been given to the nuns. The two newest gift mares were indeed glossy and fine-boned. One was pregnant, a deep bay with coal-black eyes.

"They are coursers, more or less, but smaller. Ladies' horses," Agnes said. I raised my brows. She smiled. "Like the Norman ladies and their daughters ride. Smaller bones, calm and willing and swift. Irishmen like the smaller horses for pulling light carts as well. They need less feed. I looked at Dannsair. Her sire was heavy-boned, but her dam had been tall and slender.

"Come see what we are building," Ann said, tugging at my hand. She and Agnes led me across around a wide field planted to oats.

It was their barn. The timbers and palings were set in for a long byre. "We will have twenty stalls inside for foaling mares," she said. "And a place to store winter feed. We need to learn about foaling, of course."

"I know how to help a mare foal," I said, without knowing I was going to say it. Once I had, Ann and Agnes both turned to look at me.

"I do," I said. "My mother's father taught her."

"No one here knows much about it," Ann said. "My father would not let me see or learn about it." She reached out to touch my shoulder. "If you could help me learn when the time comes, I would be grateful."

I didn't know what to say. The difficulty was the same here as anywhere. When the bogberry began to wash out of Dannsair's coat and her winter-moon color showed again, the Baron of Athenry and his men might spot her.

Once they did, there would be trouble for these women, who were being so kind to me. The baron might refuse to help the nuns if he thought they had known they were hiding a thief—and that had to be how he thought of me. And they would take my Dannsair from me again. I sighed. "Perhaps," I said.

The next day, I was put to work with six others daubing walls. Covering a new wall with the thick mix of mud and straw was hard. Ann and a nun named Fyna taught me to keep my palm flat and follow the flat-bone screed as a guide as I spread the gritted mud.

By noontime, I had improved. By nightfall, we laughed together, walking along looking at my day's work, seeing how rough my first stretch of wall was compared to my last. None of it was all that good. A dark-haired girl named Catherine, dressed in a plain leinte, was the best of us all.

"Don't make light," Fyna scolded Ann for teasing me. "It's hard work even if she is terrible at it." Catherine promised to help me improve. That set us all to laughing again.

It was only the calm and serious face of the abbess at supper time that settled us down. Still, while the abbess wasn't looking, Fyna laid a pea on the end of her knife and flipped her wrist. The pea hit me squarely on my nose.

ৠ ৠ ৠ

"I want to ask you about your filly," Agnes said, five or six days after that.

I caught my breath.

"Agnes!" one of the other nuns called. We both turned. "Mora has hurt her wrist again and cannot do her part milking."

"Coming!" Agnes shouted back. Then she touched my shoulder. "You met us on our way back from Athenry town. We heard about the race there," she added, her eyes fastened on mine.

I tried very hard to look puzzled by what she had said, but she waved one hand, dismissing my pretense. "A man who sells us cheese told the abbess a story yesterday. He said that the filly who won the race has disappeared. He told us that the missing filly's dam was from over the eastern sea." She paused and looked at me for a moment. "I don't know where you got her, but that filly is unlike any horse I have ever seen."

I had no idea what to say, so I said nothing.

Agnes gestured toward Catherine and another dark-haired girl gathering hens' eggs. "We have others who live here who have no religious vocation. Some of them are escaping cruel families or starvation. We respect the silent place inside each person. No one betrays their trust or tells their secrets. We wouldn't betray yours."

My eyes flooded with tears. They might let me stay, but it was wrong. I had no right to bring them trouble, and I was not far enough from Athenry to pretend it would never come. Nor did I want to lose my Dannsair.

That night, I barely slept. Near dawn, with the half moon still up, I decided to stay awhile longer, then leave. As much as I wanted to stay forever, I could not.

After a fortnight or so, when the moon went full, I began taking Dannsair out on the road for her gallops. I went early, before travelers would be on their way, and I was careful. Dannsair loved it. She half reared once I was on her back, then pranced as I rode her out of the pasture and up the winding path toward the road.

Her coat was still quite dark with bogberry dye, and I wore the blue-green dress for the same reason I had all along. It was the best disguise I had, should we meet anyone looking for a moon-colored filly and an Irish boy.

The horse byre was progressing, everyone helping all they could, and I always made sure I did my share and more. I wondered once if Cormac's father would consider giving a horse or two to the nuns. He was wealthy enough to be generous. I hoped the abbess would be able to meet him one day and ask him.

I turned westward onto the road as usual, to have the blinding light of the rising sun behind us. Dannsair rose into a canter, and I let her go, galloping, both of us pulling in great, long breaths of the soft morning air.

Once she had calmed, I pulled her back to a canter. It was so lovely to ride my filly through the green countryside. I thanked the old gods, the faeries, and all the saints for helping us find a place where we could rest.

And I asked them to help me make the decision to leave. I knew I had to, but it was hard. In the short time that I had been there, I had come to love Agnes and Ann and Catherine. I wanted the abbess to meet my mother. I knew they would be friends.

My thoughts collapsed as I heard shouts behind us. I cantered Dannsair off the road and headed for a thick stand of oaks—but it was too late.

Men were coming out of the woods from the north, riding a breakneck gallop in a wide fan that put some of them in front of us and some behind. I jerked Dannsair to a halt so abruptly that she reared as the riders passed on either side of us. They were crossing the road at an angle, then disappearing into the woods.

They were Normans, but their tunics were different than any I had ever seen in Athenry. Not one of them looked left, right, or behind. They were whipping their horses along. I sat, breathing hard, staring after them, wondering what in the green, wide world would have made them ride like that. I cantered Dannsair back onto the road, intending to start back to the abbey, then I carried my wondering one stride farther.

Whatever it was that had scared the Normans, it was probably still chasing them.

The instant I thought it, I wheeled Dannsair around, pressing my heels into her sides. She leaped into a canter, and I could tell that she was as uneasy as I was by the way she flattened into a real gallop without any further urging from me.

Irishmen, riding hard and armed for war, burst from the north side of the road galloping toward us.

I reined in as they came on, meaning simply to pull Dannsair to the side—and to a halt—to let them go past, chasing their Norman enemies. The last thing I wanted was to be in the way of a battle, small or large. I brought Dannsair to a plunging halt and watched them coming.

Then the two riders leading the way slowed a little and I saw one raise a hand to shade his eyes. It was only then that I remembered I was riding a Norman woven saddle and wearing a fancy blue-green Norman dress. I did not look like a poor Irish boy anymore. I looked like a wealthy Norman girl. I sat, stunned into stillness by my own foolishness.

Then I let Dannsair's reins out a little and shifted my weight forward. "Ride!" I said, using the command she had learned to start the race.

She sprang into a gallop, then lengthened her stride, digging in with her hooves. I glanced back. The riders were coming after me now.

I leaned forward a little, letting Dannsair speed up, keeping her on the road, where she could gallop flat out without hurting herself. I let her out and moved my weight forward over her withers. She understood instantly. This was a race.

The men chasing us began to whip their horses and shout, but they could not gain on us. Dannsair and I rounded a long bend in the road, and I kept glancing back, hoping desperately that they would remember their real purpose and leave in pursuit of their enemies, but they did not.

Scared, I leaned farther forward, hitching the long dress up to my knees to balance my weight just behind Dannsair's withers, the way the baron's stablemaster had taught me, so that my weight would not slow her down.

When I looked back again, the Irishmen were slowly falling back.

They could only think that I was the daughter of some wealthy Norman lord. Maybe they thought they could trade me back to my family for money or some other favor. There was no way to know, but this much was clear: They meant to catch me.

If they did, I would be able to convince them I wasn't Norman just by opening my mouth and speaking. But they might steal Dannsair anyway. She pulled at the reins and flattened out, her neck low and her muzzle extended. I let her go.

I am sure she could have outrun all the horses behind us, but we rounded another bend and I saw riders ahead of us, too—a line of men and horses blocking the road. Their weapons were drawn and their faces were fierce, and it took twenty beats of my fearful heart to recognize the man on the tall bay courser.

My father.

CHAPTER FIVE

❧ ❧ ❧

We galloped today with other horses chasing us.
None could catch me. My mother was scared,
but the men were not dangerous after all.

*I*t was all clear as rainwater in that instant. My father had planned an ambush for the Normans, but they had been wise enough to travel off the road. I, on the other hand, had ridden straight into his trap.

I pulled Dannsair back, even though she fought the bridle, still scared of the men pounding up behind us. I saw an ugly, cruel grin on my father's face as we drew nearer and Dannsair slowed to a nervous canter. That grin marked my heart forever—to see him pleased to be scaring a Norman girl half to death.

The grin was followed by a slack-jawed expression of complete astonishment as he saw my face.

Then he laughed his rich, deep, raucous laugh.

"Do you not recognize her?" he shouted to the men.

I pulled Dannsair to a full halt, and she stood uneasily, pawing and sidling as the men all leaned forward to get a good look at me.

"Larach!" Bebinn's father shouted, and they all took it up, shouting my name as though I were returning from battle. My father swung down from his horse and tossed the reins to a young man I did not know—then I recognized him. Trian! The youngest of my brothers, only six years older than I. He was so changed. His face was harder, more angled than before he had been fostered out to live with another tuath. He looked like a man now.

"And Fergal?" I called to him.

"He is well," Trian shouted.

All the men were laughing, watching me as I circled Dannsair, trying to calm her. My father strode forward, reached up, and pulled me off Dannsair's back. I looked over his shoulder to see Bebinn's father take Dannsair's reins.

My father swung me in a circle. "Where have you been?" he demanded, setting me back on my feet. "Where is Fallon?"

"It is a long tale," I said.

"Best to tell it as we ride, then," he said. "There are Normans nearby."

I nodded. "I saw them. They crossed the road long since, headed almost due north."

My father patted my head as though I were a hound that had guided a boar to his spear. Then he helped me back on Dannsair, and Trian rode to join us, riding side by side, westward, heading home.

❧ ❧ ❧

I told them both most of what had happened to me, starting at the beginning. "Our stolen gray mare was left to die near high pasture," I began. "I found her there and helped her give birth. I saved the foal, but the mare died."

I saw my father glance at Dannsair, and I

nodded. "Yes. This is the gray mare's foal. She is a lovely silvered white, but I dyed her coat brown with bogberry."

My father arched his brows, and I kept talking.

I told him about raising Dannsair, then skipped quickly through my time in Conall's barns except to say that Fallon had stayed there and seemed happy—that I was sure she could come home when she wanted to.

I left out that I liked the son of a rí who was his enemy. Nor did I tell him that my aunt Fallon loved that boy's older brother. Fallon could fight her own shouting matches with my father if she was still set on marrying her Brian. I had no such hopes about Cormac or any other boy—and I wasn't sure I wanted any. The nuns had purpose and happiness without that kind of love.

"But Fallon is well?" my father demanded. "Free to come home when she will?"

"She is," I assured him. "I stayed in the barns with the filly, but she had the hospitality of the house of the rí. We were treated with respect," I added. "It was the filly they wanted, not us."

He smiled at that. My father is like a rooster in

his pride. He was glad to know the rí had extended proper respect to his sister and daughter because it meant *he* was respected.

"The rí claimed the gray mare?" he asked.

I nodded. "He said she had been brought from across the sea."

He looked thoughtful. "I knew she was rare blood when I found her. And she was mine when she had her foal."

I nodded, understanding his reasoning—he thought Dannsair was his. I went on with my story, hoping that by some miracle, there would be no war to settle things between my father and Cormac's.

When I said I had been to Athenry, as well, my father laughed aloud. "My sons are brave and true, and even my daughter has courage," he said, loudly enough for everyone to hear.

The men cheered him, then fell silent again when Trian put up one hand. He wanted to hear the rest of the tale.

I told them about Dannsair's beautiful sire and the rí who owned him trading Dannsair to the baron. Then I described myself following the baron and his men, all the way to Athenry town.

My father stared at me as I spoke, and I had to look away to keep my mind on my tale. I could not remember ever having his attention so fully upon me. Trian was watching me, too, grinning when I told him I had used his name to pretend to be a boy and work in the stables. My father frowned at that part. My cheeks flushed when I described the race and how I had been betrayed.

"And the stablemaster promised you the horse if you won?" my father asked me.

I nodded. "He said the baron agreed and gave me his word." My father's face tightened, and I knew he was angry. "The baron is known to be a man of his word—far better than most Normans."

I finished my story quickly. I told him about Niall warning me, Old Brigit giving me her wedding dress, and how I had dyed Dannsair's moon-colored coat dark with bogberry.

"And so we rode right out the North Gate," I finished. "And no one knew us. No one even noticed us. We have slept in the woods since, and that is the end of my tale." I closed my lips, and I hoped I was not blushing. I did not like lying, but

I would not tell my father anything about the nuns. It was clear that he had no idea that there was an abbey nearby, and I planned to keep it that way. I wanted, more than anything, to go back to them one day.

My father laughed aloud at the ending of my tale.

Trian grinned at me. When he smiled, I could see his boy's face still, which lightened my heart.

"We looked for you," my father said. "No one could so much as give us a direction, and those hills are plowed with cattle tracks."

He then leaned back to look carefully at Dannsair. "She carries desert blood?"

I nodded. "The gray mare was from across the eastern sea. Remember the scar on her jaw?"

He nodded. "It was a strange way to mark a horse."

"The sire is Irish-bred," I went on. "He is the prize of the stables where I spent the winter. Her true color comes from him—it's like the face of the moon on a cold night."

"And they are raising warhorses?"

I hesitated, startled that he knew. "No one

there talked to me much," I said. "Perhaps Fallon will know."

"I have heard talk about it," he said. "The rí is lord of a number of tuatha, I was told. If it is who I think it is, there is old hatred in our families."

I didn't say a word. What he said matched what Cormac had told me.

"I knew the gray mare was a rare animal," my father said. "That's why I saved her." Then he gestured at Dannsair. "I knew the foal would have great promise."

I did not react. Dannsair's dam had been skinny and battle-wounded when he had brought her limping home. I was the one who had nursed her back to health, and I was the one to notice before anyone else that she was with foal.

I have known this all my life: My father and the truth are not strangers, but they are rarely close companions.

He was shaking his head. "It was very clever of you to dye her coat. Your mother always gathers bogberry while the weather is still cool. You will be able to keep her brown as long as I think it necessary."

"I was not going to come home," I said. "I did not wish to put my tuath in danger. And I still don't want—"

"I can protect my family," he interrupted me. I could hear the irritation in his voice. "We have won every battle since the weather turned!" he shouted. A cheer went up from the men.

My father shook his head and lowered his voice. "No one should have promised you the horse," he said. "I don't like a man who lies."

I looked off to the hills, then back at the road. Every year of my life he had promised my mother that he would be home long before he actually appeared. Every year she had been afraid for his life, for all our lives if something happened to him. Every year he had promised to stay home—then hadn't.

"We'll have to keep her close," he said, looking at Dannsair. "She is valuable."

I nodded. He was right. Horse stealing was not rare among the Irish tuatha. The justiciars did not forgive theft except in war. But most men would not complain to the courts. My father would have taken our horses back from the men who had stolen Dannsair's dam if he'd been able. And he would have taken a few of the mounts as well, to teach them a lesson.

I wondered if my father would want to turn Dannsair into a warhorse. I knew he might. He did not approve of girls and women riding at all, unless it was necessary. And a swift horse was prized for carrying a man to war. Maybe my father would want to buy armor and fight like a Norman one day. Cormac's father and Conall thought it was a good idea. If Dannsair grew heavier, he would want her, I had little doubt. If she stayed slender, perhaps he would not.

Here is the odd thing:

For all my worries, for all that I missed the abbey and my friends there, I found my heart was light and my spirits rising like a morning sun.

I was on my way home.

CHAPTER SIX

✷ ✷ ✷

My mother is happy. I can hear it in her voice. There is an
old chestnut gelding who stands close to me at night to help
me stay warm. None of the horses are as fast as I am.
My mother has me shorten my stride when we canter.

I cannot tell you the joy that rose in my
heart two days later when I first saw the
huge circle of the earthen walls of our ancient
rath. I had not known I was so close—the road I
had stumbled upon must have slanted southward.
How I loved that old rath, built by our ancestor's
hands and sheltering us still.

My father and the other men held their horses
in until we were at the base of the gentle hill, then
let them gallop. I was careful to stay well behind
them, holding Dannsair in. It was not easy. I had,

after all, taught her that when other horses gal-loped, she was expected to pass them if she could.

I kept my weight well back, sitting straight as we started up the long slope. I held the reins tight. Dannsair tucked her muzzle into her chest, pulling hard with every stride. I spoke to her, rubbing her neck, and she finally gave in and slowed.

I had my reasons for staying behind the others. I would not have my poor mother thinking my father had kidnapped a Norman girl. And I wanted her to see my father first, to know that he was all right before she had the shock of seeing me again. She always worried so when he was off fighting. And she had counted me lost and gone, my father had said.

They all had.

It had been a full a year since Conall had marched me off with Dannsair, then still wob-bling on her spindly legs.

As I cantered behind the men, I heard my mother's voice. She was calling to the other women to come greet their men, home from battle. There was a high-pitched chorus of glad shouts as I reined in, still at the rear of the procession of weary men.

I watched my mother swept from her feet as my father swung her around, his strong arms around her waist. Then he set her down and she went to embrace Trian. I saw him lean over and say something close to her ear.

Her whole body jerked, and she spun to look for me, running before she had spotted me, angling toward me once she had. I slid off Dannsair and met her midstride, both of us weeping.

Oh, it was good to see my mother again.

Oh, it was, it *was*!

I was so happy I could not speak a single word to her for a long moment. I felt so many things, all at once, that I could not master my voice.

"I have missed you so," I finally managed. "Every day that has passed, I have missed you."

That set us both to crying harder all over again. She kept stroking my hair, and I knew she was wondering why it was shorter, not longer, than when she had seen me last.

People were gathering, running across the meadows, everyone calling out, happy as they always were when my father and their own men came home.

"Larach? Lara?"

I heard Bebinn's voice and turned to see her standing beside her father and mother, staring at me as though she was seeing a faerie in broad daylight. She turned and shouted at Gerroc, and they both ran to embrace me.

Bebinn was still the tallest of us, but not by so much as a year before. I had grown and Gerroc had, too. I saw Trian talking to Tally, who smiled at me, his kind heart showing in his eyes.

My father and the men took their horses to the rath to graze and rest. I walked Dannsair behind them, waiting to see if she was uneasy being separated from me. She was not. She seemed entirely happy to be turned loose inside the earthen walls with the other horses. Inside the rath, the grass was knee-high. When my father and his men—and their horses—were gone, it always grew tall.

I spent the rest of the day answering questions and telling parts of my tale over and over. My cousin Magnus sat close to me, smiling. He was taller and stronger now, his limp less pronounced.

He had grown handsome and less shy. He leaned forward to hear every word of my story.

He wasn't the only one. Everyone listened closely, especially the women. I saw the wonder on their faces as I described Athenry Castle, the priory, the soaring stone walls, the market square with foods of all kinds, cloth, fineries, and the beautifully delicate bone combs.

It was odd to know I had seen more than any of the grown women in my tuath. The men traveled, of course, to fight the Normans or our Irish enemies, but women rarely left the tuath where they were born unless they married a fostered boy and went to live with his family.

As night fell and the new day began, people went home to their own hearth fires. It was only a little chilly, so Bebinn, Gerroc, and I sat together on the bench my father had carved from a tree trunk years before.

I wanted to tell them both about the abbey, but I did not. If I had, the whole tuath would have known before long. It is impossible to have a secret within the tuath. I had not told them about the little gold pin I had found so long ago, either.

Two secrets. I had two now. It felt very strange, and I shivered.

"Are you and Tally still taken with each other?" I asked Bebinn.

She nodded. "We are. We are both too young to plan a wedding, my mother keeps saying, but she likes him. And his mother likes me very much."

"All the mothers like you," Gerroc said. "There isn't a family in the tuath that wouldn't welcome you."

Bebinn touched Gerroc's cheek. "The same is true for you," she said, looking at Gerroc, then past her at me. "But they won't get her. Our Gerroc will be going home with Artt one day, I think."

I felt my eyes widen. "Artt?"

Gerroc nodded and exhaled a long, loud breath. "His tuath sent him here to learn bone carving from Cellaig."

"He has been here most of the past year?" I asked.

Gerroc nodded. I could see her cheeks flushing even in the firelight. "He came not long after you were—after you and Fallon were taken away."

"And you like him?"

She nodded again. "Very much. You will meet him soon. He was here when you first arrived, but you know Old Cellaig."

I nodded. Cellaig was kind-natured, but he was very serious about his work. Any apprentice would be kept busy.

I stood up suddenly, not knowing I was going to do it. "I am weary," I told Bebinn and Gerroc. It was true, but there was something else. Some feeling of distance I could not name.

Bebinn smiled and stood to touch my cheek. "Will you come help us milk in the morning?"

I nodded. Milking had been our chore since our hands had grown big enough for the task. I had not milked cows at all in a half year, I realized—nor had I missed it.

It astounded me to realize that it had been so long.

"Good night," Bebinn said, and kissed my cheek. "We are so happy to have you here where you belong."

Gerroc hugged me hard enough to bruise my

ribs. "We were all so sad that first day, running home without you . . . and . . ."

"It was terrible," Bebinn finished, when Gerroc's voice stuck.

"You helped me," I told her. She had been captured the year before, but she had made her way back to us by keeping her wits and her courage. "I remembered your courage, and it helped me to find my own."

We embraced again, all three of us, swaying back and forth for a long moment before we stepped back. Then they disappeared down the path into the dark, and I went in to curl up by the hearth, inhaling the familiar scent of my mother's herb baskets.

She had left a woolen blanket folded on the floor rushes in my usual sleeping place and had placed an everyday leine on top of that. I missed my thick woolen cloak and my own soft leine—all my possessions were at the abbey.

I had no doubt that Agnes and the abbess would wonder what had become of me—that they would worry. I knew also that they would keep my carry sack safe; the gold horse-shaped pin and the cloak would be there when I returned.

I could hear my father snoring, and I listened to the rhythm of his breathing as I lay there, waiting for my thoughts to quiet so that I could sleep.

Trian's pallet was beside the far wall, and he came in much later, moving quietly so he would not wake anyone. I wondered where he had been. Was there a girl here he liked? Or maybe he was just watching the stars and thinking. He had done that as a boy. I could remember Mother standing at the doorway and calling him to come in out of the dark.

I felt my home, my family, my tuath sleeping close and warm around me, and even though I no longer felt as if I belonged there, it quieted my uneasy heart. Eventually I slept.

CHAPTER SEVEN

❀ ❀ ❀

These high rings of earth stop the wind.
They mute the sounds of the wolves in the distance.
The horses are content here, and we all sleep soundly.

The next morning, I woke with a start, my heart leaping when I opened my eyes.

I *was* home. It had not been a dream.

My mother rose and came to kiss me on the forehead, then blew the embers back to life and rekindled the fire. She began boiling barley water. My father lay with his hands behind his head, staring up at the ceiling while my mother worked.

Trian rose and went out without speaking to any of us, his eyes still narrow from sleep.

"He is not happy here," I heard my father say. "He misses the sea, I think. He will want to go back soon."

I heard my mother sigh, but she did not answer. I shook the straw from my hair and went out into the cool morning darkness.

"I am milking this morning," I called back through the doorway.

"Don't tarry," my mother said. "I will welcome your help planting the woad and madder. Do you hear me?"

"I do," I said loudly, then turned back to look at the sky. My mother had work for me. I was home indeed.

The sun was just rising when I ran to the rath. As they had the night before, the enormous rings of earth I had known all my life seemed unfamiliar, impossibly huge. The old oak tree beside the gates rustled in a little stir of a breeze. I had hidden in its branches more than once when Fallon or my father was angry with me.

The gate seemed easier to reach, easier to open, then I realized that I had grown taller since last I had opened it.

Once inside, I called Dannasir's name softly and heard her whicker. "Dannsair?" I called again, a little louder, and I heard her moving toward me.

As she came, I could hear some of the other horses waking up, switching their tails. Then Dannsair was beside me, her warm breath tickling my cheek, my ear, my scalp. Once she was finished sniffing me, I hugged her, feeling the warmth of her coat seep into my skin.

"This is the place I told you about," I said as she nuzzled me. "This is home."

Dannsair lifted her head sharply, and I knew she had heard something. A few seconds later, I knew what it was. I could hear Bebinn and Gerroc talking as they came up the path.

"I will come back later," I promised Dannsair. "I have to go milk now." I kissed her warm muzzle and hugged her once more.

"There you are!" Bebinn called when she saw me coming out of the tall gates of the rath. She and Gerroc had been heading up the path to my mother's house. They turned and headed toward me.

I ran to meet them.

Bebinn hugged me hard. "Oh, Larach, how we feared for you."

Gerroc nodded. "We wept nearly every day."

Bebinn touched my cheek. "We were afraid you would be beaten or not fed enough—and we were sure that the filly would be stolen from you. We knew that would break your heart."

I fell into step beside them, walking the paths that I had walked every day of my life, until the past year.

"Was it terrible?" Gerroc asked. "You said no one hurt you. But how could you stand to be away so long, so far from everyone?"

"It was very hard," I said, answering carefully. I could see from her face that the very idea of being anywhere but here terrified her. Had I ever felt like that? I wasn't sure. I didn't now. But she wanted to go with Artt one day, I was sure. She would have to find the courage.

"I was just trying to take care of Dannsair at first," I said aloud. "Then I was trying to find her, then, finally, running away, trying to take care of her again."

"And you couldn't come back without her," Bebinn said.

I nodded. "I believed that I couldn't ever come back at all without bringing danger with me. The baron might still look for Dannsair."

Gerroc was staring at me. "He might?"

I nodded. "He will hate the idea of being bested by an Irish boy. If he talks to the rí or to Conall and suspects I am a girl, he will be even angrier."

Gerroc was frowning. "You thought you would never come back?"

I nodded.

I saw their faces change. Bebinn pushed her wild red hair back from her face and looked away.

Gerroc couldn't imagine never coming home, I knew. Bebinn was probably scared by the idea of angry men coming to the tuath. She reached out and took my hand without saying anything for a long time. Then she turned to face me as we walked. "When I was captured, I was gone from home only a few days. And no one was cruel to me. Your courage had a far greater test."

Gerroc was walking in silence, listening to us.

She had never been away from home, I knew—no farther than high pasture last summer. She had never been taken away by strangers, unsure how she would be treated. She didn't know something that Bebinn and I had both found out.

This is the truth:

You think you don't have the strength to survive terrible things. But you do. We all do. How else would the generations go on, one after another?

I was lost in my own thoughts when Bebinn laughed aloud.

I turned to look at her.

She smiled, crinkling up her eyes. "I just remembered—you don't know who went to summer pasture this year, do you?"

I shook my head.

"Guess."

"Who?" I hadn't given it a single moment's thought, but of course someone had gone as always. The cows were moved the day after Beltaine so that they could get fat and have their calves in the soft new highland grass. With them gone, the grain fields could grow untrampled.

Bebinn refused to tell me so I finally named the two older girls who had gone with us the year before. "Dailfind and Inderb?"

"Yes," she whispered, "with six *boys*, all of them fourteen or fifteen, close to grown."

Gerroc nodded. "It's true. Your father was afraid to send girls by themselves after what happened to us last year."

I exhaled. Boys Trian's age at summer pasture? They probably hated it. There was nothing to do sun to sun but milk, strain curds, and press cheese. Dailfind and Inderb would be needed to teach them—few boys ever learned anything about dairying.

I could hear the cows gathering in the dawn-dusk around the gate of the little dairy byre as we got closer. We went inside. Bebinn used the red-hot coal she'd brought from her mother's hearth to light a strand of oat straw—then used that to light the fat tallow candle on the shelf above the spancels.

An enormous black-and-white cat slipped into the door and rubbed against my leg.

"It belongs to Magnus," Bebinn said. "He fed

it from a cloth dipped in milk. Its mother disappeared—wolves, probably. It was the runt of the litter and look at it now."

I laughed. It was the biggest cat I had ever seen. It was easy to imagine Magnus playing mother to a kitten. He was gentler than most boys—than most girls for that matter.

Milking felt odd. My hands ached when we were finished—in all my life that had never happened. And there were only five cows in the byre to milk. The rest had been taken to high pasture where the grass would be tall and thick.

We picked up our heavy pails and started for home.

"The manuring was almost our chore again," Gerroc said after walking in silence for a time. "Now, with the men home, we will only have our mothers' gardens."

Bebinn nodded. "And all three gardens won't take more than a day or two. Then we can spin or go bee hunting."

"I'll help manure," I promised. "My mother is thin again, and I don't want her doing any hard work."

"She has been gray-faced and sad over you and your father," Bebinn said.

I glanced back at her as I walked. Her words had struck at my heart. I had not thought of it that way, though I should have. I had watched my mother worry her way through the spring and summer months all of my life—battles were usually fought in warm weather, and my father was usually gone.

"Perhaps you should rest," Gerroc said. "You had a long journey."

I laughed. "I worked much harder staying in Athenry than I have since leaving it." I held out my arm and tightened my muscles.

"Better than most boys," Gerroc said, and we all laughed.

And it was in that moment that we all heard hoofbeats. We hushed, turning to face the long slope, listening.

CHAPTER EIGHT

☙ ☙ ☙

Men came today. They smelled like the place where
I was kept for so long, away from the sun and fresh air.
My mother was not with them. I stood behind
the chestnut gelding who grazed near me.
I have no wish to go back to that place.

*S*ix horses burst out of the trees. I stared;
my worst fears had come true. The riders
were wearing Norman tunics and leggings, and I
recognized a heavy-boned piebald gelding from
the Baron of Athenry's barns.

"Get home," Bebinn said, nudging me. "We'll
go tell our fathers."

I turned and ran, hearing shouts behind me in
the same instant. Bebinn and Gerroc wouldn't
have to tell anyone. The whole tuath had heard
the riders coming.

I was nearly home when the men galloped past me, reined in, and shouted my father's name. He came out and stared up at them. Then he noticed me and gestured. "Get the milk inside, daughter."

I nodded and closed the door behind myself, then stood beside my mother, quivering with fear. I had managed to scan the faces. I knew none of them—and that was a blessing. The stablemaster had not come.

My mother patted my hand. "They thought you were a boy."

I nodded. "Only Old Brigit knew, and she would not tell."

My mother pushed my hair back out of my face. "Then you are safe. They are looking for a gray-white filly."

I nodded, hoping she was right. They would not recognize Dannsair—she was grazing among twenty or thirty other horses.

"Or maybe," my mother whispered, "maybe they just want supper and a place to rest."

I nodded, not sure what to hope for. If they were looking for Dannsair, they might soon leave, satisfied she was not here. If they had come to claim their right to hospitality, they might stay a day or two, eating the best of our scant food. They would want guides to help them hunt boar or deer. They would sample our mead and sit at my mother's table, talking long into the night. I shivered, thinking about them staying that long.

I opened the door just far enough to peek out. What I saw made my legs tremble. The Normans were riding behind my father as he led the way to the rath on foot.

So, then. It was what I feared.

They were here to look for a moon-colored filly. The Baron of Athenry had sent them. I held my breath and my mother's hand as two of the men followed my father through the tall gates. I could not see what they were doing inside the earthen walls, of course. Whatever it was, it seemed to take more time than it should.

Dannsair's coat was still bogberry brown—Old Brigit's dye had worked very well. But if they walked through the horses, they might notice Dannsair's long legs, her height—she was far too tall for a common-blood yearling. Her head and neck were finely cut, too, graceful beyond any horse I had ever seen.

I looked across the wide meadow past the rath at the houses beyond. I could see Gerroc and Bebinn and Trian—and almost everyone else—pretending to work.

They were really watching.

Everyone knew about Dannsair and me, of course. They had all heard the story. They all knew, and not one would ever tell. I was sure of that. Oh, how I wished they would stop watching so closely. It might make the baron's men suspicious.

After what seemed like a fortnight, the Normans came back out of the rath. I could hear them laughing with my father. I felt my mother squeeze my hand. My father closed the tall gates and stood talking to the men for another long moment. Trian walked toward them, and my father gestured for him to come close. I could tell that he wanted my brother to learn something of the Normans.

My father played this part so well. He hated the

Normans, and he fought them when he could, just far enough from home to go unrecognized. But to their faces, to the Normans who ruled us, he was charming.

After another moment or two, the Normans all turned their horses at once and cantered back down the hill. At the bottom, I heard one of the horses at the back of group coughing on the dust they had raised.

Trian and my father walked home in long, quick strides, both of them grinning.

"Larach?" he said as he got closer. "There is nothing to fear. They are just going from one tuath to the next. They won't be back."

I came out of the door, my relief too great for words. My father lifted me off my feet and swung me around. "They can't tell one Irishman from another. They aren't sure whether we fight them, or only feed them."

"I hope you're right," I said quietly, surprising myself by saying it at all. My father was not used to people doubting him.

His mouth tightened into a straight line. "Of course I am." He patted my head, and I knew his thoughts were already elsewhere as he turned and walked away. Trian patted my shoulder and smiled at me, then followed him. I realized, watching Trian walk away, that I had lost him in a way. He was nearly a man now, absorbed in my father's concerns, not my mother's or mine anymore. It made me sad.

My mother came out and stood beside me. "I heard," she said. "I only wish the battles would end so he could stay here with us. So they all could."

I put my arms around her and held her for a long moment. It felt odd. My whole life, she had comforted me, and she would have then if I had voiced my real worry—that there would never be anyplace I could live without bringing danger to people I loved.

When she straightened, I released her and stood back. "Gerroc and Bebinn say we are to manure gardens today. May I? Please?"

She smiled, then she laughed aloud.

So did I.

I had sounded like a little child begging for a sweetmeat.

"I just want to be with Gerroc and Bebinn," I

told her when our laughter had subsided.

She nodded, still smiling. "I know. They have missed you terribly. They both came to see me, each and every day. But . . . you plead with me to go *manuring*?"

I grinned and nodded. I felt giddy, foolishly happy. The baron's men had come and gone. I was safely home, and my friends were waiting for me as ever they had been, all my life. I wanted to pretend that was enough, that my life was settled and happy, I suppose.

Manuring was great fun, if you can believe it.

We let Dannsair pull the rawhide drag. She didn't like the leathern breastband and cinch at first, but she wore it to please me and was steady and calm by noontime, walking willingly from the dairy byre's manure piles to the gardens, pulling the flat rawhide drag, piled high with fertilizer.

Bebinn and Gerroc patted and praised her, too. The year before, we had been the ones dragging the heavy load. Bebinn made a great show of kissing Dannair on her muzzle. We all laughed. It was barely work at all.

Even so, the gardens took three days, not two,

because on the middle day it rained. We ran to my house for shelter. We knew that my mother was at Old Orlaith's little byre of a house. She helped the old woman whenever she could, grinding her herbs into dye powders, stringing her loom. Better still, we knew that my father—and theirs—were off hunting deer.

It was wonderful to be alone, just the three of us, after being so long apart. We spent the afternoon laughing and talking—and spinning, so no one could accuse us of idling.

My spinning had improved, both Bebinn and Gerroc said so immediately. I told them more about Old Brigit in Athenry, her incredible weaving and dyeing skills. I showed them the Norman saddle she had given me for my escape from Athenry. It was old and worn, but beautiful still.

Bebinn ran her hands over the thick, padded roll that fit over the horse's withers. "How did she *do* this?"

I shook my head. "I watched her do it, and I am still not sure," I said. "She used a loom unlike any I had ever seen." I described the double-layered warp as best I could. They had both already admired the bridle I had made for Dannsair. I explained tablet weaving as well as I could.

"I wonder if people across the ocean weave differently than we do," Gerroc said. She looked up at me. "Are there many different peoples across the ocean?"

"I don't know." I met her eyes and saw something strange pass over her face. "What are you thinking?" I asked her.

She blushed. "That you have seen things I will never see."

I did not answer immediately. She was right. I had thought almost the same thing. "Not because I meant to," I said after a silence. "It was all an accident."

"No it wasn't," Bebinn said, laying down her spindle. "Most girls would have run. They would have hidden and wept while a Norman baron took a filly they had raised. You didn't."

"It's true, Lara," Gerroc said.

I went back to my spinning and spoke without looking at either of them. "Dannsair thought I was her mother. She still does. And I love her. I could not let strangers take her away from me."

"Still," Gerroc said. "You were the one who followed the Baron of Athenry. You found a way into his city!"

I shook my head. "That was Niall's help, nothing I did on my own."

"But you *were* on your own," Gerroc said stubbornly. "And no one told you what to do. How many girls ever experience that?"

I nodded, unable to think of anything more to say.

She was right.

We were all quiet for a good long time after that. I am not sure what they were thinking, but I was admitting something to myself. For all the danger, the loneliness, the miserable cold and hunger, I had *liked* being off on my own, answering only to myself. I liked being able to have a secret now and then.

We fell back to our spinning and raced one another, laughing when Bebinn dropped her spindle trying to go too fast. I boiled weak barley water, and we sipped it from my mother's horn cups, pretending we were royal Norman ladies. I told them about the beautiful dresses I had seen the Norman girls wear. They wanted to see Old Brigit's gown again, and I showed them. They sighed, feeling the soft cloth.

"Tally says your father asked him to ride Dannsair tomorrow," Bebinn said carefully.

I turned to face her, sure I had heard wrong. "My father asked . . .?"

She nodded. "He asked Tally to give Dannsair a good gallop tomorrow. I thought you might mind, and I told Tally so. He says he is bound to do what your father tells him."

I stared at her. "Why would my father need Tally to ride her?" I asked, looking up at the timbers in the roof.

Bebinn sighed. "I knew it would bother you. I am sure Tally will be gentle with her."

I bit at my lower lip. "I am not sure she will let anyone else on her back. She threw a mean-hearted Norman boy in Athenry." It was true. I wasn't sure, even though Tally would be gentle. But that was not what made me so uneasy.

I didn't want anyone else riding Dannsair, at least not yet. She was young, and Tally was much taller and heavier than I. But that wasn't the whole reason.

Dannsair was mine, not my father's. But I had known he would not see it that way. I had hoped to convince him over time. Bebinn watched me for a time, then went back to her spinning.

"Was Tally waiting for you after supper last night?" Gerroc asked her, finally breaking the long silence.

"He was," Bebinn said. "And he was upset that I had to work so long that it was dark out and we could not go walking."

"Artt is impatient in the same way," Gerroc said.

And so Bebinn and Gerroc began talking about Tally and Artt. I hadn't told anyone about Cormac, but it wasn't that keeping me quiet. I realized, listening to them, that this was what they talked about *most* of the time now.

I had had the courage to follow my Dannsair, to save her and bring her home. But I had missed a hundred talks like this one. My friends were closer to each other than they were to me, now, and knowing that made my heart ache.

CHAPTER NINE

🐎 🐎 🐎

My mother came early while the sky was just getting light.
We galloped a long course. It felt wonderful.
The air was soft and cool.

𝒯ally did not ride Dannsair the following day. It was not that my father had changed his mind. I did not speak to him about it at all. Instead, I got up at dawn and bridled her and gave her a good gallop before anyone else was awake.

I kept to the paths below our rath, and was careful not to go too far, in case my father woke early and saw me. He was a late sleeper when allowed, my father. But that morning, he rose earlier than usual. Perhaps he heard Dannsair's hoofbeats.

I did not see him come out into the morning sun until I was walking Dannsair to let her sweat dry.

He waved one arm above his head. "Larach!"

I trotted her up the hill, my hand tight on the reins, my mouth dry. "Yes, Father?"

He scowled at me. "What are you doing?"

"I don't want Dannsair to lack for exercise," I said quietly and evenly. I could feel my own pulse.

"You have other work to do," he said. "Proper work for a girl."

I knew what he meant. He meant that my riding a horse was wrong, that horses should belong to boys and men, not girls.

"I have been doing my work," I said politely. "And I spun wool with Gerroc and Bebinn the day it rained," I added, meeting his eyes. He scowled at me, and I looked away. "Mother saw what we did and thanked us for staying busy when we might have been idle."

There was a long awkward silence between us.

"I have taken care of Dannsair since the day she was born," I said, and managed to keep my voice even, which surprised me.

"Do you expect my thanks?" my father demanded. He looked at me as though he was seeing a stranger. It was the oddest feeling. I thought about the abbess, about how she kept everything in order without telling anyone how to think or feel—and I kept my lips closed. Arguing with my father is pointless.

Finally, he cleared his throat and gestured angrily at the hillside. "You are not to ride her out of sight of the rath. And stay out of the forest."

I knew he was thinking of my safety. I opened my mouth, meaning to tell him that she was fast enough to outrun almost any kind of trouble. But I did not say it.

"Thank you," I said quietly. "I will keep her fit."

"If you can do it without missing your proper chores, I will allow it," he said.

I nodded, trying to look grateful, not angry and insulted, which was what I was feeling, to be honest. I had always done my share. What bothered me was his thinking he was the one to decide who rode my filly.

I know that sounds foolish.

Of course my father had every right to tell me what I could do or not do. All fathers had that right—and he was rí as well as my father.

But I hated it. There is no softer way to say it.

I hated that he was the one to decide, not me. I knew it would not be much longer before I had to leave or he would be training Dannsair for war. If I went back to the abbey to get my clothes and the pin, it would be difficult to leave. I sighed. All I wanted was a place to be safe, where I would not bring danger.

From that morning onward, I fell into a habit of waking while it was still pitch-dark and the stars were glittering overhead. I would leave the house, careful of the door latch, tiptoeing until I was out. Then I ran, following the long path to the rath.

Every morning I inhaled the sharp scent of the oak tree, the soft woolly smell of the moss on its bark. Every morning, I got on Dannsair and sat still, talking to her, patting her neck until it was light enough to bridle her and lead her out.

Then, while everyone else slept, we raced invisible horses, the clouds, the wind. After the first few mornings, we took the same course each time, a long circle that followed the line of the woods downhill, crossed the wide meadow, then wove around two massive old oaks and crossed the creek before starting back up the gentle hill again. Dannsair's hooves began to wear a path in the soft soil.

In my tuath, and in all tuatha, I think, the paths are old. Ours had been worn by the feet of our ancestors and the hooves of their cattle, back hundreds of generations. The oldest ones were like broad, flat-bottomed ditches, lower than the earth around them.

With every morning's gallop, Dannsair and I deepened and widened the strip of churned earth along our route. Then it began to pack down hard. I didn't think about it until Bebinn was telling Gerroc where to find a patch of deep grass to restuff her pallet. Lice had gotten into Gerroc's bedding.

"There is standing bedstraw from last year between Larach's path and the edge of the forest at the bottom of the hill," she said, gesturing. "Just this side of the two oaks."

Gerroc nodded, and they went on talking.

It didn't seem to strike either of them strangely, but it bothered me. I had never met anyone who had a path called after them. It felt wrong, like one more thing that made me different from my friends, from all the girls of the tuath.

For a few days, I took a different route, but the one we had fallen into was really the best, so I went back to it.

The next day, I boiled bogberry powder and mixed it with spoiled barley flour and darkened Dannsair's coat again. While I was leading her in circles, waiting for the dye to set, Trian came out and sat on the old bench.

"I leave tomorrow," he said.

I turned to face him. "When will you be back?"

He shrugged. "I don't know. Father will tell me when to come, I suppose."

"Mother misses you," I told him.

He sighed and nodded. "I know she does. And I miss her and everyone else but . . ." He looked at me. "The tuath where I am fostered is bigger than ours. We work hard, but the rí there loves music. Irish and Norman bards visit, the girls make feasts, and we dance and sing. The rí is less . . ."

He stopped and I could see him fishing for a word.

"Angry?" I said.

He nodded. "They don't hate the Normans. There is a Norman girl who came with her father once . . ."

He trailed off again, and I wondered if he ever finished a thought. I was going to tease him, until I saw the look on his face and realized what he had said. A Norman girl. Our father would never allow him to love a Norman girl.

When Trian left the next morning, he embraced me for a long time. I wished him good fortune and watched him ride away. My mother and I stood until they were out of sight. Then my mother went into the house and closed the door. I heard her weeping, and so I left her alone.

A few mornings later, at the end of our morning gallop, Dannsair coughed. I had never heard her cough before, and it startled me. She shook her head and I thought she had inhaled a fly or a bit of seed-down. But then, as I was putting her back in the rath with the other horses, she coughed again.

I was still not concerned, until I remembered the horse from Athenry coughing. Still, Dannsair was as fit and muscled as any horse I had ever seen, young or old. She had gone well that morning, had been hard to hold in, as usual. Perhaps dust flung up in our galloping had bothered her throat.

I spent the rest of that day helping plant the last of our barley fields. It was an odd-shaped field that my father had decided to clear and plow because we'd had a good crop of seed barley one year and he hadn't wanted to waste any of it. We had more seed than usual again this year—so he told us to plant it.

The men had plowed, of course. So the heaviest work was done. Two of us scattered the seed while the third dragged a squared log back and forth to bury it.

We took turns, starting at the high end of the field. I took the hardest job first, following along behind Bebinn and Gerroc, dragging the heavy log over the seeds they had scattered. Then Gerroc took the leather strap and pulled the log, leaning into the weight.

It was slow work. By the time it was Bebinn's turn, it was sprinkling rain and the sun was going down. Since we had to stop before we finished, we began again just after sunrise the next day. I put off riding Dannsair to do my part.

In the lower half of the field, the ground itself was difficult, full of stone. Then men had plowed it, of course, but they hadn't carried out the rocks. Every winter seemed to bring a few more to the surface.

We began by carrying them one by one to the edge of the field, staggering under the weight. Then we wrestled them uphill to the loose stone heap of a wall that had been growing a little taller every year between the field and the forest.

Midmorning, Bebinn called out to me. "We could carry the stones to the edge of the field so Dannsair's hooves won't tear up the plot, then she could pull the drag the rest of the way."

I exhaled and thought about it. The hill wasn't very steep. I was pretty sure the rocks wouldn't roll off the rawhide drag. "I'll go get her," I called back.

I ran home to get Dannsair's bridle and the leathern breastband and cinch we had used when she pulled the manure drags. At the rath, I opened the gate and spotted her instantly, her lovely, fine-boned face placid as she turned to face me.

Then she coughed. She stretched out her neck, shaking her head, her breath rough.

For an instant I was scared that whatever dust she had breathed before had settled inside her lungs. My heart stumbled in my chest, and I felt cold fear seep through my whole body. Then my father's bay stretched his neck out and coughed, and the fear tightened inside me like drying rawhide.

A mare close to the earthen wall coughed, too, more softly, but still a cough. Then I heard a rasping sound off to my right.

I ran to Dannsair and put my arms around her neck. Her body felt too warm, and she leaned against me a little, the way she had when she was a foal and overtired.

I bit at my lip, trying not to cry.

The horses were sick.

My Dannsair was sick, her eyes dull and feverish. I shook with fear as I ran to get help.

CHAPTER TEN

❧ ❧ ❧

I feel tired, as though I have run a long way, and I hurt.
What is this enemy that attacks without teeth or claws?
I cannot breathe without pain.

I ran.

I ran first to tell my mother, pulling at her hands, begging her to let me know what herbs we needed, pleading with her to tell me how to help my filly.

"Horse-cough comes on fast," my mother said calmly. "A few will die of it. Most will not if they get the medicine soon enough."

That brought me to a stop. "You know about it?"

She nodded. "I have seen it twice; anyone my

age has. Fallon was little the last time the coughing sickness came—you weren't yet born. The
sooner we draft the horses, the more likely they
are to live through it."

My mother was refastening her brat pin as she
spoke, then walking toward the baskets lined
along the wall opposite the hearth. "Cattle can get
it, too," she said. "I have some dried heart's ease
flowers from last year for a start. Build up the
fire. We need to fill the iron pot with water and
get it boiling."

I ran to blow away the thick layer of white ash
so that the coals lay bare. I used a twist of oat straw
and raised a little flame. Adding the kindling
carefully, my hands shaking with worry and hurry,
I soon had a crackling fire.

My mother helped me lift the pot into place
and we filled it with the fresh water my mother
had carried from the creek at sunrise—as she
always did.

"Where's Bebinn's father?" my mother asked
me. "He's a good hand with horses."

"I don't know," I told her.

"Probably off with your own father, hunting

boar," she said. "All of them are, I imagine." She exhaled loudly enough for me to hear her breath.

I nodded, handing her the basket of dried flowers when she pointed at it. She looked older than she had when I had left—a lot older. Was it her worry over me that had taken away so much of her spirit? I hoped not. Oh, I hoped not. I loved my mother.

"Did the men go on foot?" she asked.

I nodded. "I think so. I didn't count, but most of the horses are here. Father's tall bay is. They might have led one or two to carry the meat home."

She nodded. "If the ones they took start coughing—and they probably will—your father will be home quickly. If not, we might not see him until tomorrow or the next day." She smiled at me, one of her quick, fading smiles.

"It's fortunate most of the stock isn't here," she said.

"It is," I agreed, grateful to talk about anything that kept my mind from my fear for Dannsair.

My mother smiled a thin, tight-lipped smile. "Maybe they won't get it. We can hope—and later we will light a candle and ask Saint Brigid to protect our beasts."

I nodded. Our brood mares and yearlings—any horse not needed over the summer for plowing—were at high pasture.

"Run and ask Tally to come talk with me," my mother said abruptly, shooing me with both hands. "I need a boy who can listen carefully. Don't tell anyone else just yet. I want time to think."

I tore off down the path, running as fast as I could. Tally was breaking flax for his mother, but he came. My mother met us in front of the house.

I heard my mother explaining to him how to make medicine for the cough. Then she had him repeat it back three times to make sure he had it right. I listened closely. There was a good deal to remember—it wasn't just heart's ease flowers.

Then she told Tally to run to high pasture—going on foot. "Tell them to listen for coughing and, if they hear it, make the medicine and draft the cows as best they can. Keep them grazing if they can. Some starve because they don't feel like eating."

Tally nodded.

"If there is coughing, tell them to throw away the last five days' milk and cheese and keep throwing it away until no cow has coughed for ten days," my mother said sternly. "Tell them to eat no meat, milk, or cheese from the sick cows—it carries the poison of the disease. People can die from it."

Listening, I caught my breath.

I had been so concerned about Dannsair that I hadn't thought about much else. What would we do if we could not eat a whole summer's worth of milk and cheese? People would surely starve over the winter. No milk, cheese, or meat? What could we possibly—

"Larach," my mother said sharply. "I will need your help."

I stared at her, realizing that Tally had already gone. I could see him running, halfway back to his mother's house.

"Stop frightening yourself," my mother said. "It helps no one and will only make you less able to do what you need to do. Learn that early in your life if you can. You will need it more than once."

I nodded, embarrassed that she had to take her mind off her own thoughts to calm me. I followed her through the door of our house. She led me through part of the preparation of the medicinal draft. The heart's ease flowers had to be bruised by rubbing them between your hands. The water had to boil, then subside to a steaming simmer immediately, or the medicine was ruined. We set the bucket of steaming infusion outside to cool.

"I need the other herbs, and we will be running buckets up and down the hill all day long," my mother said, pressing her hands into the small of her back. "Go tell everyone we need their help."

"Are you certain the medicine will work?" I asked.

"Nothing is certain in this life," she said, patting my cheek. "Now go."

Bebinn and Gerroc were coming up the path, wondering why I was taking so long to harness Dannsair and find a drag to use. I explained, breathless, and we scattered, running different directions to find everyone at their different tasks. Magnus knew where to look for the boys herding pigs in the forest. Artt ran to tell the sheepherders.

I was the one to tell Old Orlaith. She patted my cheeks with her shaking hands. "I am too old to carry buckets or gather herbs," she said. "But tell your mother I will light the candles and plead with our Saint Brigid."

The entire tuath walked up the hill to listen to my mother. By the time I was on my way to the rath with the first cooled bucket of the infusion, I could hear, behind me, my mother shouting directions and descriptions of the herbs she needed. She sent some of them off to the woods to find more heart's ease flowers and a lichen that would cleanse the horses' bellies. Others were sent along the creek for cress and willow bark.

I saw Magnus running off with the others, his lopsided gait nearly as swift as anyone else's. He had always been like that—had always worked harder than most.

He saw me looking and waved, his face somber. He knew how much I loved Dannsair. I remembered what Bebinn said about his feeding the newborn kitten. He probably understood how scared I was.

My heart heavy with cold fear, I opened the rath gates. Dannsair looked up and whickered at me, then she coughed. The deep grating sound of it terrified me, but I tried to stay calm for her the way my mother had stayed calm for me.

Dannsair was eager to drink and didn't seem to mind the taste of the flowers in the water. She drank nearly half the bucket before she lifted her head.

I offered what was left to my father's tall bay. He drank most of it. The rest I gave to Bebinn's father's sorrel mare. Then I went to stand with Dannsair for a moment.

"You will get well," I promised her. "You will." And it was only then that I cried. Dannsair stood close to me, her head down, her breath brushing my ankle. She coughed again, long and hard. I hugged her and wiped my eyes and picked up the bucket.

On my second pass down the hill to the rath, I braided the forelock of each horse that had had enough of the infusion. Walking back, I told the others to mark any horse that drank its fill the same way. The next day, we would *un*braid those that had had their fill. I saw my mother's approving glance, then went back to work.

Everyone who was able helped carry the buckets. By midafternoon every horse had had a long draft of my mother's medicine.

We were standing in a ragged little crowd, all breathing hard from carrying buckets, when my mother clapped her hands together. "Now we prepare for the morrow. If we make the second batch now, we'll be able to give the next draft early in the morning."

No one complained.

We all went back to making more of the infusion, adding the other herbs this time. The lichen had to be pounded into a mealy powder. The willow bark was added while the water was still boiling and left there for a time before the bruised flowers were put in, then the water was allowed to cool to a simmer for a time, then taken off the fire entirely. Once it was cool enough to dip a finger in without flinching, the lichen meal was added.

Most households had an extra bucket or two. We filled them all with the infusion and then set them in a long row to cool along the side of the house.

Once we were finished, we all stood back, glancing down toward the rath, all of our eyes straying in that direction, like sheep drifting toward a creek on a hot day. I tried to stop looking every time the faint sound of a horse coughing reached my ears, but it was hard.

"Is there nothing else I can do for Dannsair?" I asked my mother when everyone had gone home.

She shook her head. "Not now. Later, when the sun goes down, you can take a blanket down and cover her. Damp and chill help with no illness that I know."

"I am so afraid for Dannsair that I feel weak," I whispered. She put her arm around my shoulders.

"Tomorrow, we'll make some leek broth for Dannsair and your father's horse. I don't have enough for all. Maybe some of the other families dried leeks last year. I hope so. I told them it might help."

Then, before I could say anything more, my mother patted my head, kissed my cheek, and walked away, her shoulders rounded forward, her step slow.

Later, at sunset, just before the new day began, I took a thick woolen blanket to the rath and laid it across Dannsair's back. My mother had given me leather thongs and I gathered up the two front corners and tied them together.

On a usual day, I would have been concerned that she would get tangled up in the blanket and tear it, freeing herself. But she was truly and terribly sick. She would not be moving much this night.

I went back to the house and got a second blanket, then told my mother I was going to sleep beside my filly. I saw her brows arch, but she didn't say anything. I suppose she could tell from the look on my face that she could not talk me out of it.

"I slept with Dannsair to keep her warm the night she was born, and every night after that until the baron took her away," I said, trying to explain how I felt. "She was so little and she would shiver . . ." My eyes filled with tears so suddenly that I had no chance to blink them back.

My mother nodded. "You are feeling what any mother feels."

"It hurts," I said.

She nodded again. "Sometimes it does."

"I am sorry," I said quietly. "For being such a worry to you."

She pushed my hair back from my eyes. "If it starts to rain, come back to the house. Bring the mare up here if you must, but don't sleep wet."

I hugged her, then went back out into the dark, following the path to the huge gates. Dannsair was glad to see me. After a time, she lay down heavily. I pulled the blanket straight, tugging it up over her withers. Then I wrapped myself in the blanket and lay down beside her, pressing against her side to give her a little warmth, one arm over her neck.

CHAPTER ELEVEN

❧ ❧ ❧

*All the horses are coughing now. It hurts and it frightens
me to have my very breath bring me pain. My mother
is often beside me. It calms me and I am grateful.*

It is hard to describe how my fear for
Dannsair clouded my heart. The next
morning we all carried the full buckets to the
rath. Dannsair drank hers eagerly and even ate a
little grass when I offered it to her.

She was still listless and carried her head low—
and she still had the racking cough—but I was
encouraged by her eating.

After Dannsair was settled, dozing in the
morning sunshine, I went with Bebinn and
Gerroc to milk. We were all listening, hoping and

praying that we would not hear cattle coughing. We did not. And so we took the milk home and I clabbered the curds to make soft cheese, leaving my mother and me only the whey to drink.

She looked at me and smiled. "Yes. Let's keep making cheese with each day's milk. If the cows get sick, we will have food for a time anyway." She smiled at me. "You are growing up well, Larach."

I looked down at my bare feet, then met her eyes. She rarely praised me, and when she did, it lifted my heart. "Are we going to make leek broth for Dannsair?" I asked her.

She nodded. "And for your father's horse."

We set to work. I cut up the leeks—they were shriveled and dry, but none had molded. My mother turned them often and set the baskets by the hearth fire.

My father's horse tasted the broth and turned his upper lip inside out, shaking his head. We could not make him drink it, so Dannsair got his share, too. It seemed to me that her eyes were a little brighter and that the cough was less coarse. I slept beside her again that night and the next two, rising early enough to help with milking.

It was chilly the third morning as we walked to the little dairy byre, and the sound of the creek made me shiver a little.

"The cows seem all right," Gerroc said as she blew on the glowing coal she had brought in a little iron box. When it was bright, she used it to light a twist of straw. "When will our fathers be home?" she asked, carrying the burning straw to the shelf to light the candles.

Bebinn shrugged. "My mother said they were hunting boar."

We fell silent while we milked. We were all tired. Carrying the buckets of water was heavy work, and we had to go farther and farther to find the herbs.

"What if..." I said slowly, while we were rinsing out our milk pails in the creek. "What if the cows do get sick? What could we do?"

"I heard what your mother said," Bebinn answered. "Mine says it, too. Last time the horses coughed like this, anyone who ate meat or drank milk from a sick animal got sick. We would have to find other food."

No one said anything to that. There *was* no

other food this time of year. The barley was planted and growing, the oats were up, but we were a whole, long summer away from harvest.

"My mother and I are making cheese every day," I said.

Then we all fell silent again. As odd as it sounds, we three, who talked constantly, had nothing more to say. We were all tired, and we were all scared.

Dannsair seemed a little better again that day and the next. I brought her the heart's ease medicine and leek broth each morning and each evening, and she drank it all. On the sixth day, I led her out of the rath and let her graze along the path, walking her slowly. She was still weak, but the cough was subsiding.

"You're going to be all right," I told her. She nuzzled my cheek, and I rubbed her forehead.

The next morning, after milking, I ran back to the rath. Dannsair was up, standing with her head low, which scared me until I realized that she was grazing. My father's bay looked better, too; he was holding his head higher.

And then I spotted Gerroc's father's old

chestnut gelding. He was lying awkwardly, his neck stretched out and this muzzle resting on the grass. He had been doing better each day, too; they all had. Somehow, his sickness worsened.

All I could think for a long moment was that he looked uncomfortable, that it was an odd position for a horse to sleep in. Then I finally realized that he had died.

I bit at my lower lip. He had been an old horse, nearly twenty, and he had been around all of my life. He was quiet and gentle and never caused trouble of any kind. And he had stood close to Dannsair most nights. My eyes stinging with tears, I ran to get my mother and she walked back with me—then we both went to fetch more help.

It was a terrible day. Everyone in the tuath had a story to tell about the old horse. Magnus had learned to ride on him. Several of the boys had, and they all remembered falling off and the gelding waiting patiently until they dusted themselves off and got back on.

We finally used an ox hitched to a makeshift drag to pull the gelding's body slowly out of the rath, down the wide path we called the Cattle Road, and then a little ways into the woods.

While we had been getting the harness straight and making a drag big enough, the boys had been digging. We pulled the chestnut's body alongside the lip of the deep hole, then we had to line up to push him in.

As we worked, the ox startled us all by coughing. It belonged to old Orlaith. She had walked with us even though she could not help much. She stepped forward, her hands fluttering uncertainly. The ox coughed a second time, and everyone started talking at once.

My mother held up one hand, and we all quieted. "We have a great deal to do," she said. "We will all miss this good old gelding. He always worked hard and steady, and we must do the same. Some should finish here," she gestured to the gelding's grave. "Magnus can lead the ox to the rath to be kept apart from the other stock. The rest should go back into the woods and gather heart's ease flowers and the other herbs. We must keep making the draft."

For a moment, there was a scatter of voices as

people discussed how to go about the job. I heard Magnus and Artt arguing about who should go in which direction.

Then we all fell back into silence as we set about our tasks. No one was singing or joking. Burying a kind old horse and fearing sick oxen and cattle kept us quiet.

My mother and I built four fires outside to help the hard work of making the draft go faster. We borrowed Bebinn's mother iron pot and Old Orlaith's. The boys carried them to us, stopping to rest a dozen times on the long path.

We were all weary. My arms ached as I worked, and I wondered if my mother's did. If so, she hid it well; she worked fast and took no extra rest.

The boys took turns tending the fires as a way to rest from hauling water buckets up the hill. It was Magnus's turn when we heard voices. "It's your father," Magnus called as I came up the hill with a full bucket.

I turned to look.

Magnus came to stand beside me. "But who is that with him?"

CHAPTER TWELVE

❧ ❧ ❧

One of us is gone, the kind one who often grazed near me.
The rest are better. The grass tastes almost sweet again,
and most of the heaviness has left me.

*M*y father was leading the way. Behind him were Bebinn's and Gerroc's fathers leading two horses burdened with meat—a stag and a boar. The others followed on foot.

I stared at them and held my breath.

No. How was this possible? Cormac and his father—the powerful McDonagh rí? Did my father no longer consider him an enemy? Then I saw who was behind them and I had my explanation. Cormac's older brother walked close to my aunt Fallon, holding her hand. She still loved her Brian, that was plain to see.

Had my father approved his sister's marriage to an old enemy's son? It certainly looked that way. They were all smiling and talking. My father, at the head of the party, was strutting like a cockerel at sunup.

I stood helpless, trying to think what to do. This rí, father of Cormac and Brian, was the one who had taken Dannsair from me and traded her to the Baron of Athenry. He knew about the race—he had been there with his sons and Conall, his stablemaster, to watch it. Surely he knew the filly had disappeared.

It made my knees weak and my thoughts spin to see them all at once. How could I ever manage to escape? Dannsair was still not strong enough to travel fast, was still drinking the drafts of medicine every day.

My father laughed loudly and said something back to the rí. Cormac's father was wearing rich, Norman-style clothes, his breeches and tunic a clear, sunny-yellow color. I could only imagine his reaction to my father's old leine, belted with leather at his waist, our little tuath, our clean little byres.

My father was smiling as he came closer. Had he given even a moment's thought to my safety or Dannsair's? The nuns kept one another's secrets. My father had no such concerns. Had he told them all my story? All the long, weary way I had come, and now I might very well lose my filly again. Cormac's father might very well insist on returning her to the baron, hoping for a gift of gratitude or some other favor.

Cormac spotted me and made a gesture of greeting. I lifted my hand slightly, my heart pounding in my chest. Well. There was one good thing. The bond between Brian and Fallon seemed to have ended the old enmity, stopped the battles. There would be one less enemy for my father to fight. And Cormac and I could be friends, perhaps.

"Larach?" my father called out. "Fetch your mother!"

"I am here," my mother shouted back at him, startling me. I turned to see her walking into the clearing, setting down her bucket. She faced downhill, her hands on her hips, her breathing quick and deep. Others came up behind her and set down their pails.

"Have you brought us guests on this day of all days?" my mother said, too softly for anyone but me to hear her. Then I saw her eyes widen when she recognized Fallon.

I told her quickly who the strangers were. Her eyebrows arched, then flattened. I watched Cormac's father talking to mine as they came toward us. "Do you think Father would tell them Dannsair is here?"

She shrugged wearily. "Maybe. If he has, it is for some reason that makes sense to him, Larach." She lifted her chin and cupped her hands around her mouth. "We have had the horse-cough. Most are better now, but not all are quite well."

My father nodded. "I told you," he said to the rí. "My wife knows the cure." He looked at my mother again. "I met them on the road, coming to ask your help. Their horses are sick, and Fallon remembered that you have a cure."

I blinked. At least it all made sense now. They

had been coming here on foot because their horses were weak. Fallon came along to make sure my father didn't attack the rí before he could explain his purpose.

People of the tuath were coming up the paths from the creek and out of the forest now; they had heard the voices. Bebinn and Gerroc and their mothers came to stand close to mine. They all looked tired, but their faces were lit with curiosity, too. I heard them talking to one another, staring at the rí and his sons—and Fallon. None of them had ever seen her smiling like this, her happiness making her pretty.

As he topped the rise, my father swung my mother in a circle as he always did upon returning home. Then he turned to face the people of the tuath.

"Today we welcome Fallon home to our tuath."

People managed a faint cheer that faded quickly into a murmurous tangle of low voices. Everyone was curious, and they wanted to know more than the simple facts that any child could see.

"We welcome also the rí of the tuatha McDonagh and his sons, Brain and Cormac.

Thanks to Brian and Fallon, our tuath and theirs will soon be joined by marriage." My father pointed at Brian.

That silenced everyone. Fallon had been an ill-tempered girl who barely washed her face and who had tormented any and all with her bossiness and her anger. Of all my family, only I had seen her transform once she had fallen in love with her Brian. I hadn't told anyone, not wanting to set off a war if my father had objected. It was obvious that he did not, and I was relieved.

"Brian's father, Dáire McDonagh," my father said in a loud, grand voice, "is rí of many tuatha, known across Galway and Connaught for the horses he is breeding. His second son is Cormac." My father paused, waiting for all eyes to focus on him. "They kept my Larach safe and fed her well and have treated Fallon with honor and kindness."

I stared at him. Was this how men settled wars? By leaving out half the truth? They had fed and honored us, more or less, but they had also captured us to get Dannsair. They held us from coming home, and had finally stolen Dannsair from me to trade her to the Baron of Athenry.

The rí nodded politely when my father finished. He met my eyes for just an instant, and it gave me a chill. He knew that *someone* had stolen away from Athenry with the race-winning filly. I looked at Cormac and found him looking at me. I smiled, a tiny hard-to-see little smile, then felt my mother's hand on my arm and turned. Her mouth was slightly open, her eyes on my father, her expression somewhere between simple exhaustion and mild anger.

I knew what she was thinking. My father was holding up important work that she had spent nearly every bit of her heart and strength to manage. The horses were all better. Old Orlaith's ox was mending, and none of the others had gotten it so far.

". . . and so the old enmity ends this day," my father was saying. "We will fight no more. We look forward to a marriage that will forever heal the old wrongs."

No one cheered for a second, then someone realized we were supposed to and shouted. Everyone else joined in. Then Brian's father stepped forward, and we all tried to cheer again. It was ragged and thin. No one wished Fallon ill, I was sure. But she had never been a kind friend to any of us, really. More than that and most of all, we were all so tired we could barely stand.

I stole another glance at Cormac. He was looking around, probably wondering how a tuath could be so poor, its houses so small.

"Well and good," my mother said suddenly in a loud, flat voice. "Now we have much to do. Who will be learning the cure to carry the knowledge back?"

I saw a flicker of anger cross my father's face.

"My wife is always this eager to get back to her work," he said to Cormac's father, and most of the men laughed.

It upset me to hear him making light of my mother. If it had not been for her, he would have come home to a rath full of dying horses. I might have lost my Dannsair—and he would have had no reason to be shoving out his chest and acting important. It was, after all, my mother who knew the cure for the cough, not him.

"I can learn it," Fallon said. There was something about hearing her voice that made everyone step forward to wish her well, to welcome her home. Then they all went back to work as she and my mother went inside the house. I saw the McDonagh rí follow them after a moment. He probably wanted to listen, to find out for himself what was in the draft.

The rest of us went back to work. Brian and Cormac helped, and it was welcome. By the end of the day, Bebinn and Gerroc were giving me sly looks. I suppose it was obvious that I liked Cormac.

That evening, he found a way to sit beside me at the fire. Tally came home just before dark with good news, and we all listened as he told the tale. Only five of the horses had gotten the cough before he arrived to teach everyone at high pasture how to make the draft. They had all worked hard, keeping the horses far from the cattle—none of the cows had gotten sick.

We all cheered him. It was an enormous relief, of course. We had all been worried about the rest of our stock.

My mother and the other women managed to make a small feast that night, roasting stag meat and boar over fires outdoors so all could gather.

The stars were bright, and the weather was mild. I asked Cormac about his colt—Dannsair's half brother, who was the same moon color as their father. Cormac's face lit up, then softened into worry. "I named him *Linaid*. He is smart and very spirited. He will be a handful to ride."

I smiled. It was a very good name. It meant *a promise kept*.

"He was all right when we left," Cormac said. "I asked Conall to take special care with him, but . . ."

I nodded so he wouldn't have to finish the sentence. I could see the concern in his eyes. "My mother's draft helped every horse here except one, and he was very old. And you heard Tally. It works very well, especially if it is given quickly."

Cormac nodded and exhaled. "I like your mother."

I tilted my head. "She is one of the strongest people I know," I said, without thinking about how it might sound. "I don't mean she can carry a sheep," I added, then stopped again, blushing.

"I know what you mean," Cormac said. "My

mother is like her. She works dusk to dusk and never complains. I will come back to your tuath for the wedding," he said. "We will see each other then, at least."

"I hope so," I told him, and felt my cheeks go hot.

"I am glad our fathers have put an end to the fighting," he said.

"Yes." I looked away, knowing my cheeks had gone an even brighter pink. I was glad of the darkness and the flickering firelight.

I waited for my cheeks to fade a little before I looked back. He told me about Linaid learning to open the storeroom door to steal oats. "Dannsair is smart like that, too," I said, without thinking. Then I closed my mouth, furious with myself for bringing her up at all. I had said *is* not *was*.

"She was stolen from the baron," he said. "After the race."

I nodded, glanced at him, then looked away. "I only hope whoever has her will take good care of her."

"Oh, I think you can be sure of that." He looked at me sidelong, then lowered his voice to a near whisper. "I saw you leaving Athenry. What did you rub into her coat to change her color like that? Do you still have her? Does your father know?"

"Cormac, don't talk about Dannsair or about me to anyone," I pleaded.

He whispered an apology. "When you can, tell me," he said, "I have lain awake nights thinking about your courage. If I can ever help, tell me."

I turned to smile at him, grateful. He reached out to touch my hand, then we both stared forward again. I wanted to tell him about the abbey, about how I wanted to live there one day, if ever I could do it without bringing trouble to the nuns who had been so kind to me.

"Cormac!"

He turned at the sound of his name. It was his father calling.

"Come now to sleep. We will leave before sunup!"

Cormac leaned toward me, and I felt his lips brush my forehead. "I meant what I said about helping."

Then his father called again, and he was gone.

I walked to the rath and slept beside Dannsair that night. I was so weary from making the horse draft that I did not wake when the rí, his sons, and Fallon left our tuath on foot. I did not hear the hoofbeats that came up our hill as the sun lifted over the forest. I am sure my mother knew where I was—she simply meant to let me get a little rest.

I did not waken until I heard the gates creaking open, and I stood up, sleepy-headed, to see the baron's stablemaster staring at me. Behind him, my father looked grim and angry.

"There," the stablemaster said, pointing at me. "There's our horse thief and the baron's filly. What have you done to her coat?"

CHAPTER THIRTEEN

𝕊𝕊 𝕊𝕊 𝕊𝕊

My mother was scared, so scared that it made me uneasy.
I knew the man walking toward us. He had never been
cruel to me, but I had never liked him. I stood close to
my mother, and we waited as he approached.

*T*he stablemaster tied my wrists and led me
along. Four guards followed behind us,
one of them leading Dannsair. Next in line was
my father, his hands bound as well, his horse
being led, his temper raging though there was
nothing he could do about it. Five more guards
followed behind him.

I was glad of one thing:

Cormac had been well on his way home before
the stablemaster had arrived with the castle
guards. If he had still been in our tuath, he might

have tried to help me escape. It would have been impossible, and the last person I wanted hurt by everything I had done was Cormac.

The journey was slow and miserable. My hands were not unbound, even to sleep, so I couldn't, not more than little naps. All day long Dannsair would whinny now and then, wondering why I was not with her. I would wrench around to see her—and find that my father was glaring at me.

Now that it had come to this, he wasn't proud of me tricking the Normans anymore. He was angry because I had caused this much trouble. My mother had wept, the whole tuath had been uneasy and angry, watching my father extend his hands to be bound, saying loudly to all who could hear that he was innocent of any wrong. Oh, yes, my spirits were low. This was the exact thing I had meant to prevent by staying away from my home. I should have known they would come back.

Despite the circumstances, Athenry looked lovely in the morning mist the day we arrived. The castle appeared to be floating on a cloud, its arched windows glowing with torchlight from within.

How strange it was to be back in a place I thought I would never see again. As we rode through the North Gate, I looked back to see Dannsair tossing her head, going faster. She liked it here. She was bright-eyed as we passed through the crooked paths of the town and headed for the barns.

I will tell you true, I was afraid. I had no idea what they might do to me for stealing Dannsair. I knew they saw it that way, and there was nothing I could do to change their minds.

My father was led toward the castle. I saw him sit straighter as they neared the high walls and the enormous gate. I hoped that they were taking him inside as a matter of respect, but it worried me, too.

Dannsair and I were taken to the barns. The stablemaster got off his mount at the gate, then pulled me off the horse I had ridden, letting me stumble awkwardly.

"How did you think this would end?" the stablemaster hissed at me. "A poor Irish grub would ride away on a rare-blood filly owned by a Norman baron?"

I nodded. "I did, because I took your word."

He laughed. "So you say. I say I gave you nothing. And it is me the justiciar will believe."

My spine went cold at that. He was probably right. He nudged me forward. "Walk. No one is going to carry you." He pulled at the huge barn door, and it swung open as he turned to look at me. "I am going let you stay with the filly tonight, both of you tethered, of course. In the morning, we will get this sorted out once and for all. Your father will pay a fine or worse. And then he will teach you not to steal, I am sure."

He laughed again and took Dannsair's lead rope from the guard and dismissed the man. As he walked away, the stablemaster looked at me. "Do not run. Cause no trouble or you will be sorry. Follow me."

I nodded, wanting only to be near Dannsair as long as I possibly could be. I could not try to escape—not while they held my father. He would stay for my sake as well, I was sure.

Two things happened in that instant. I understood why they had separated us, and I heard a horse cough.

A moment after that, I saw that nearly every horse had its head down. Another rasping cough rang out. I saw the stablemaster stop, then turn, his eyes widening.

"Sir?" a voice called out.

I looked back to see one of the boys who fed the horses running toward us.

"The baron said to tell you as soon as you got back that they are sick, sir. The horses are all sick. Four have died in the past two days alone. We have lost fifteen altogether."

My first thoughts were for Dannsair's safety, but I remembered what my mother had said and my heart calmed. She'd had the cough once. She would not get it a second time.

The Baron of Athenry came into the barn. He and the stablemaster spoke in short, clipped sentences. I listened carefully.

The horses had begun coughing four days before. One had coughed, then they all had, all at once, or so it had seemed. The baron was frantic. The stablemaster was little comfort. He said he had seen the cough once before, as a boy, and most of the horses had died. He had heard years later that there was some Irish cure, but he had never seen it. Hope bloomed inside me, and an astonishing idea came into my head. It seemed a good time to raise my voice.

"I can cure your horses, sir," I said, as clearly as I could. My voice was shaking. When they turned, I looked at the baron.

"Be still," the stablemaster said sharply to me, the turned to the baron. "She is lying." He jerked at Dannsair's rope to move her into an empty stall and she reared, startled.

"I can cure them for you," I repeated. "Ask my father what we have spent the last fortnight doing in our tuath."

"What will he tell me?" the baron demanded.

"That my mother knows a draft of infused herbs from her mother that will save most horses, and that she taught it to me. My whole tuath has been making the medicine dusk to dusk. We lost only one horse, an aged gelding."

The baron shouted, and two of his men came into the barn. He explained what I had said and sent one of them off to talk to my father, who was before the justiciar, to witness what was claimed.

The stablemaster put Dannsair in a stall and pushed me in after her. He used Dannsair's lead to tie my bound hands to the railing. Then the two men walked away from me, talking.

Once they had gone too far for me to overhear, I listened again to the coughing of the horses. It was awful. They all looked dull-eyed and weary. Across the aisle was a bay mare I remembered for her high spirits. Her head was nearly touching the ground.

I was tired and worried, and Dannsair came to stand beside me. I shifted to lean against her, her warm coat much more a comfort than the wooden rails. I closed my eyes and must have dozed a little.

"Larach!" I woke to the sound of my father's shout. The baron and the stablemaster were behind him.

"Untie her," the baron commanded. The stablemaster set me free. I rubbed my aching wrists, all three men staring at me.

"If you can save them all, not lose a single one," my father said, "they will give the filly as payment."

"The justiciar agrees that there is cause to

forgive," the baron said, looking at my father.

He nodded. "I told him the mare was in foal in my possession, that I found her on a battlefield with many ownerless horses upon it. I told him I hand-raised the filly, that it would have died without care."

The baron waved a hand to quiet my father. "If this girl saves my horses and teaches my stable-master how to make the draft, I will relinquish the filly and pay you fifty silver pennies. The horses in these barns are worth fifty times that. Can she do it?"

My father lifted his head. "And on this bargain, you give your word and bond as a man, a Norman, and Baron of Athenry to me, an Irishman, rí of my tuath, and a man of honor?"

The baron nodded. "I give you my word. But only if all the horses are saved. Every one."

I bit my lip. "And if I fail?"

"You will both be free to leave. The filly will stay here."

I nodded, feeling so many things at once that my thoughts tumbled over one another. Then I remembered what my mother had said about scaring myself. I had watched her organizing the tuath all my life. What would she do next? I looked around the barn.

Ach. It was terrible. The horses breathing roughly, their eyes half closed. The air was dusty and close, as it always had been, and now there was the terrible, damp smell of sickness, too.

I took a deep breath. There was no time to lose. "I will need twenty or more boys to gather the herbs and carry buckets of the draft. Have them bring linen sacks, the bigger the better. And I will need ten more to help set up iron pots and start cookfires."

The baron gestured at the stablemaster. "You heard her. Find thirty boys. The Irish alleys have that many playing and more. Promise them a bit of food at the end of the day. Hurry."

The stablemaster went out, and the baron called his guards inside to keep an eye on my father and me, then he left.

My father followed me as I walked the barns, looking into each stall. My old friends Fothud and Guaire were cleaning manure, and they were astonished to see me and amazed to realize I was a girl. I lowered my voice and squared my shoulders to make them laugh. Then I asked for their help.

I found a length of twine and asked them to tie a piece to the stall gate of horses that had gotten sick first—the worst ones. They set off at a run.

"You are much like your mother," my father said quietly.

"I hope so," I said.

At that moment, the big doors at the end of the aisle opened, and the stablemaster came in leading a parade of boys, some as young as Magnus, some nearly as old as Trian.

My mother knew how to make people feel as if they were working together, with one heart and one purpose. I tried to imagine what she would do.

I clapped my hands together and stood as tall as I possibly could. "Listen carefully. There is much to do," I said evenly, then waited until the boys quieted. "You will have to learn quickly or we will lose another horse to the cough, and if we do, the prize will be gone."

"Prize?" one of the older boys said.

My father looked at me sternly, but I nodded

and went on. "Silver pennies. There will be one for each of you, but only if every horse lives."

From that moment on, we were all of one mind. I sent a boy to fetch Old Brigit, if she would come. She arrived just as I was leading the boys to the woods. We embraced and nearly wept with happiness to see each other. Oh, it was lovely to see her again. She understood quickly what I needed, and when I left, I knew there would be boiling water when I returned.

And so there was, the pits dug neatly, wood stacked close, and poles to lift the pots off the fires when we needed the water to cool. By nightfall every horse had had a draft—the worst ones had had two.

None died that night. In the morning, I opened the big doors at both ends of the barns. There was a breeze and fresh air washed through. Some of the worst cases turned for the better that day, so I left the doors open after that.

The piebald gelding I had recognized in the woods nearly died. No other came so close. He lay down for five days, and I covered him with blankets and pushed the bucket under his nose while the medicine was still warm. He drank it all.

Finally, on the sixth day, rack-skinny and weak, he got to his feet and started to eat. There was a cheer, and I turned to see half the boys watching. I went to cut fresh grass.

It took nine long days. I barely slept. The boys barely slept. Old Brigit was at the barns most of every day, and even my father helped, in his way. He went back and forth to the castle to tell the baron our progress, and he went with the boys to the woods to see that they gathered herbs and didn't play.

On the eleventh day the baron came to see the horses for himself. All were well; all were eating. He brought my father with him. He granted my father Dannsair, then handed him the pouch of silver coins.

My father held the pouch and turned to me. "These coins were not yours to give. But a promise is a promise."

He handed the boys their coins and we all celebrated, cheering and dancing and saying good-bye. That night, I slept *inside* the castle. Before I went off to sleep, I asked my father to give me Dannsair, to make her my own. I knew it was a good time to ask.

My father was proud of me. He liked being inside the castle, talking with the baron and his important friends. He might still fight the Normans a day's ride to the east or the north, but he wanted to be respected by them.

He patted my head. "She is your filly, Larach. You have earned her." I wanted to believe that he meant it, but I knew that he didn't, not really.

The next morning, we left.

CHAPTER FOURTEEN

❧ ❧ ❧

My mother came this morning! I am so glad to see her.
We went to gallop, and it felt wonderful.

*W*hen we got home, I began cantering Dannsair every morning as I had been before her cough. By the time Fallon and Brian were to be wed, Dannsair was entirely recovered, as fit and sleek as ever she had been. I saw my father looking at her in the rath one morning and knew what he was thinking.

I thought about it long and hard; then I told my mother that I might leave again for a time, but I would be back. Her eyes darkened, but she nodded without saying anything.

Fallon and Brian were married the old way, with dancing and music. Cormac and I found ourselves on the edge of things, and we walked toward the rath, talking. I told him the truth—that I would be leaving again soon. "You and my mother are the only two I trust with my secrets," I admitted.

"Then I will trust you with mine," he said. "I am to be fostered out in Athenry Castle—that's where I will go from here."

It took a long moment for that to sink in. "With Normans?"

He nodded. "My father wants to learn more about their ways, their armor, their swords, everything. He says the baron wants his sons to learn about the Irish."

I opened the gates and called Dannsair's name, and she galloped to me.

Cormac's eyes widened as he watched us playing. When she settled down, she rubbed the side of her face on my shoulder, and I could smell her grass-sweet breath.

"Cormac!"

It was his father shouting.

Cormac sighed. "He doesn't want me talking to you too much," he said. "He would like me to find a Norman girl to marry." He touched my cheek. "I won't, that much is certain."

I blushed. "Nothing in this life is certain," I said, repeating what my mother had told me.

He faced me. "I will help you if ever I can, Larach." He looked straight into my eyes. "That much you can count on in this life. That much is certain."

"And you can depend on me," I promised. "That is certain, too."

❧ ❧ ❧

It was not even a fortnight later that my father asked Tally again to start riding Dannsair. "I want her to get used to the weight of a man on her back," he told me, then turned away before I could argue. Then a few days later, he and the men rode away, as they usually did once the crops were in and half grown. He promised my mother that he would be back with the men to help with harvest.

I left on a warm summer night with a full moon.

First, I told my mother good-bye and explained why I was leaving. She looked into my eyes and spoke quietly. "I will keep your secret, Larach. Come back to visit me when you are able?"

"I will not be too far," I promised. "I will come when I can. Please give Gerroc and Bebinn and everyone else my love." We embraced, and we both cried.

The ride back to the abbey seemed swift and short now that I knew the way. As I rode, I thought about my mother living at the abbey one day if my father died in battle. I thought about Old Brigit, too. I knew the nuns would love them both. They were alike in many ways. They were clever and capable and loved peace and harmony.

It was just past sunup when the abbess welcomed me with a smile and an embrace. For the first time, I told her my whole story, starting with Dannsair's birth and ending with the baron's bargain and my father's promise."

"And now he wants her as a warhorse," I said. "I have not told anyone where I was coming," I added, "only that I would visit when I could."

She nodded. "We can give you safety. No

Irishman would attack an abbey, nor would any Norman. Your father might be angry, but there is little he can do if you are here. It is that way with all of us. You are not the only one with worldly troubles."

I thanked her and ran to see the others. Agnes danced a circle when she saw me. It was lovely, lovely.

I fit back into the abbey as easily as a fish slides back into a pond. I helped with everything, but I spent most of my time with the horses.

Their horses had not gotten the cough yet, but I began gathering heart's ease and the lichen and storing the herbs in baskets in my little room. I taught Agnes and several of the others how to make the drafts in case one day they needed to know.

That evening, my heart peaceful and my Dannsair standing beside me as I watched the stars, I thought about my life, about what I wanted to do with the days that were given to me.

Back in my room, my evening candle lit, I shook out the cloak Cormac had given me and hung it on a wall peg.

Then I took out the little gold horse pin I had hidden for so long. I had always been afraid that it would be stolen, or lost, or cause someone to be jealous or suspicious of where I had gotten it. Warming the gold in my hand, I realized that none of those things would happen here.

I slept soundly that night and woke to a calm silence in the morning. I rose, washed my face, and took the pin to the abbess as a gift. "I could never give you enough," I said, "but I want you to know that I am grateful just to be here, to feel safe at last."

She smiled, holding the little pin. Then she reached out and pinned my brat with it. "You are enough of a gift, Larach. We need no other. Agnes is fussing over the pregnant mare," she added. "She tells me you know something of foaling?"

I nodded.

"We are very glad to have you here, Larach," the abbess said. "You are clever and you work hard. Welcome home."

I smiled at her and went out, walking the long corridor that ran the length of the church. The arches cast beautiful shadows, and I could *hear* the complete silence of the nuns praying inside as though it were a sound of its own. It rang like bells in my heart as I ran to the pasture to see Dannsair. I called her name, and she cantered toward me.

I watched my graceful filly dance to a halt, reaching with her muzzle to touch my hair. The abbess had said it perfectly.

That was how I felt.

Like I was home.